WILD CARD

Tiki Barber and Ronde Barber

with Paul Mantell

A Paula Wiseman Book
Simon & Schuster Books for Young Readers
New York London Toronto Sydney New Delhi

For AJ and Chason—T. B.

For my three roses—R. B.

ACKNOWLEDGMENTS
The authors and publisher gratefully
acknowledge Mark Lepselter for his help in making this book.

ALSO BY TIKI BARBER AND RONDE BARBER

By My Brother's Side • *Game Day* • *Teammates*
Kickoff! • *Go Long!* • *Red Zone* • *Goal Line*

SIMON & SCHUSTER BOOKS FOR YOUNG READERS
An imprint of Simon & Schuster Children's Publishing Division
1230 Avenue of the Americas, New York, New York 10020
This book is a work of fiction. Any references to historical events, real people, or real locales are used
fictitiously. Other names, characters, places, and incidents are products of the author's imagination,
and any resemblance to actual events or locales or persons, living or dead, is entirely coincidental.
Copyright © 2009 by Tiki Barber and Ronde Barber
Football signals on pages 149-156 created by Einav Aviram based on NCAA rules
Copyright © 2009 Simon & Schuster
All rights reserved, including the right of reproduction in whole or in part in any form.
SIMON & SCHUSTER BOOKS FOR YOUNG READERS is a trademark of Simon & Schuster, Inc.
For information about special discounts for bulk purchases, please contact Simon & Schuster
Special Sales at 1-866-506-1949 or business@simonandschuster.com.
The Simon & Schuster Speakers Bureau can bring authors to your live event. For more information
or to book an event, contact the Simon & Schuster Speakers Bureau at 1-866-248-3049 or visit our
website at www.simonspeakers.com.
Also available in a Simon & Schuster Books for Young Readers hardcover edition
Book design by Krista Vossen
The text for this book is set in Melior.
Manufactured in the United States of America • 0915 OFF
First Simon & Schuster Books for Young Readers paperback edition July 2012
4 6 8 10 9 7 5
The Library of Congress has cataloged the hardcover edition as follows:
Barber, Tiki, 1975–
Wild card / Tiki Barber and Ronde Barber, with Paul Mantell.
p. cm.
"A Paula Wiseman Book."
Summary: Through the course of a difficult season, Ronde learns that his coach is right
about football being a mental game, as he tries to fill in as kicker while he and his
identical twin, Tiki, help Adam improve his grades.
ISBN 978-1-4169-6858-0 (hc)
[1. Barber, Tiki, 1975—Fiction. 2. Barber, Ronde, 1975—Fiction. 3. Football—Fiction.
4. Twins—Fiction. 5. Brothers—Fiction.] I. Barber, Ronde, 1975– II. Mantell, Paul. III. Title.
PZ7.B23328Wil 2009   [Fic]—dc22
2008046641
ISBN 978-1-4169-6859-7 (pbk)
ISBN 978-1-4169-9657-6 (eBook)

EAGLES' ROSTER
8TH GRADE HIDDEN VALLEY JUNIOR HIGH SCHOOL

HEAD COACHES—*"SPANKY" SPANGLER (GRADE 7), SAM WHEELER (GRADE 8)*
DEFENSIVE COACH—*PETE PELLUGI*
OFFENSIVE COACH—*STEVE ONTKOS*

QB
CODY HANSEN, GRADE 9
MANNY ALVARO, GRADE 7

LB
RICKY RUSSELL, GRADE 9
GARY, LITTMAN, GRADE 9

RB
JOHN BERRA, GRADE 9
TIKI BARBER, GRADE 8

WR
FRED SOULE, GRADE 9
JOEY GALLAGHER, GRADE 9, HOLDER

OL
PACO RIVERA, GRADE 8

CB
RONDE BARBER, GRADE 8
BILL REEVES, GRADE 9*

DL
SAM SCARFONE (DE), GRADE 9

K
ADAM COSTA, GRADE 8

CONFERENCE SCHEDULE

WILLIAM BYRD JUNIOR HIGH BADGERS—GAME 1 (HOME) — L 20–21
PATRICK HENRY JUNIOR HIGH PATRIOTS—GAME 2 (AWAY) — L 7–14
MARTINSVILLE JUNIOR HIGH COLTS—GAME 3 (HOME) — W 48–3
NORTH SIDE JUNIOR HIGH ROCKETS—GAME 4 (AWAY) — W 31–28
PULASKI JUNIOR HIGH WILDCATS—GAME 5 (HOME) — W 38–3
MARTINSVILLE JUNIOR HIGH COLTS—GAME 6 (AWAY) — W 34–17
BLUE RIDGE JUNIOR HIGH BEARS—GAME 7 (HOME) — W 30–10

REMAINING GAMES

JEFFERSON JUNIOR HIGH PANTHERS
EAST SIDE JUNIOR HIGH MOUNTAINEERS
BLUE RIDGE JUNIOR HIGH BEARS
WILLIAM BYRD JUNIOR HIGH BADGERS
NORTH SIDE JUNIOR HIGH ROCKETS

CHAPTER ONE
SAVING THE DAY

"THEY'RE GOING LONG, RONDE!"

Ronde Barber heard the warning, shouted by his twin brother, Tiki, from the sidelines.

Like he didn't know. He was already backpedaling as Harrison Hochberg, star receiver for the Jefferson Junior High Panthers, ran straight at him.

Hochberg's red number 99, outlined in bright yellow, stood out from the black of his Jefferson Panthers jersey. 99—as in "miles per hour." Ronde knew he had to keep pace, because this kid was *fast*. Really fast.

Was he going to deke first, or would he just put it into high gear as he got by Ronde? To stay with his man, Ronde would have to guess, and guess right.

Just like that, Hochberg's eyes flicked back toward the line of scrimmage for an instant. Most cornerbacks would have taken it as a signal that the ball was about to be thrown.

But Ronde was too smart for that. He knew it was third and long, with only ten minutes left in the game.

1

He knew that the Panthers, with only a two-point lead, would be looking for a big gainer.

He didn't jump at the bait, and when the receiver kicked it into high gear, Ronde stayed with him step for step.

He didn't look back for the ball—not yet. He remembered Coach Wheeler saying, during one of their team video sessions, "You can't keep up with someone fast if you're looking behind you."

Ronde kept his eyes squarely on number 99. He waited till Hochberg turned his head to find the ball. When the receiver's eyes grew as wide as saucers, Ronde finally turned, knowing the ball was about to arrive.

His hands and the receiver's hands reached out together. There was the ball! Ronde reached even higher . . .

Suddenly his feet were caught up with the feet of the receiver! They both went down in a heap, tumbling over and over each other.

"Interference!" number 99 yelled, getting back up and pointing at Ronde as he hopped up and down in frustration.

"No way!" Ronde said. "I was going for the ball!"

But the bright yellow flag was already sailing through the air, the whistle was blowing, and the ref was pointing straight at Ronde.

"It was incidental contact!" Coach Wheeler yelled from the Eagles' sideline. "No foul!"

Of course, it didn't matter what Coach Wheeler, or Ronde, or any of the Eagles said. The ref was the law, and he was motioning to the kids with the chains to come fifteen yards downfield.

"First down, Panthers!" the ref said. He blew his whistle again, and pointed to the Eagles' end zone.

Ronde sniffed back the hurt and bit his lip hard. It was so unfair! He'd known what was coming, he'd played it perfectly—and how did he get rewarded? With a flag!

"Come on, come on!" shouted Mr. Pellugi, the defensive coach. "Get back in the game, Barber!"

Ronde jogged back to the huddle, but his heart was still out on the field, where it had just been stomped on by the ref.

"Bad call, yo," said Bill Reeves, the Eagles' other corner, patting Ronde on the back. "Never mind. Let's stiff 'em now."

Ronde nodded, shaking off his emotions. It didn't matter how bad he felt. He had a job to do, and he meant to do it, no matter what.

He watched his man line up, and thought, *I'm gonna bump him right out of this play.*

But the Panthers' receiver never came past the line of scrimmage. Instead he waited until the quarterback faked a handoff, then rolled out. Hochberg got into blocking stance and came straight at Ronde.

Now the tables were turned. Ronde tried to avoid the

hit, get by his man, and reach the quarterback. But just as he was about to make a tackle, he was slammed to the ground with a hard hit from his right!

He was still lying there when the roar went up from the Panthers and their fans.

TOUCHDOWN!

Ronde just lay there for a minute, panting. He was in pain, but his pride was hurt worse than his body. Now the Eagles were behind by nine points—30–21—with less than ten minutes left to play, in a game they *had to win*!

The truth was, they were *all* must-win games from here on out. The Eagles had already lost twice this season—in the first two games. One more defeat and it would take a stroke of incredible luck to get them into the play-offs.

If they wound up missing out on the postseason, it would be the first time in seven years that a Hidden Valley Junior High team didn't make the play-offs.

The shame of it would be hard to bear, Ronde thought, dragging himself over to the sideline and practically falling onto the Eagles' bench.

"Get back out there, Barber," Coach Wheeler barked at him. "Kickoff's coming. Or are you too out of breath to return it?"

"No, no, I'm okay," Ronde assured him, forcing himself to get back up off the bench and into the game.

"'Cause I can get someone else to run back the kickoff . . ."

"I'm going! I'm going!" He swallowed hard. "Coach, I didn't—"

"I know you didn't foul him, Ronde," Coach Wheeler said. "But that's how it goes sometimes. You don't always get the breaks."

Ronde sighed, and nodded. He knew it was true.

"But, hey—on this team we pick each other up," Wheeler said. "Keep the faith, son. Let's get us a win here."

Tiki came up to him and put a hand on his shoulder. "Hey, no worries, Ronde. We're gonna pull this one out. You'll see."

Ronde looked back at his twin. It was the same face he saw in the mirror every day—they were so identical it was hard even for their close friends to tell them apart.

But there was a difference right now. There was hope in Tiki's eyes. Ronde had never felt more defeated in his life.

"Come on, man, give me the handshake." Tiki held out his hand, waiting for the secret ritual shake they'd made up over the course of the season.

Ronde just sighed.

"Come on, come on!" Tiki demanded. "No time for losing!"

Ronde nodded. Tiki was right. There were still nearly ten minutes left. Plenty of time to make up for that penalty—plenty.

"Go get 'em!" Tiki told him as they gripped fingers, tapped knuckles, then snapped their fingers twice before slapping five low, then high.

Ronde ran back out onto the field, buckling the chin strap of his helmet. He waited for the kickoff, ready to do something to turn the game around. *Tiki's right,* he told himself. *We can still win this thing. And we will.*

Up went the kick, low and end-over-end. It hit the ground, then bounced off to the left, far away from Ronde. He ran after it in a panic, and got hold of it just in time to get piled on by the entire Panthers kicking squad.

"Great. Just great," Ronde muttered to himself as he trotted slowly back to the bench. The ball was spotted at their own fifteen—a long way from the end zone.

Now the Eagles lined up on offense, and Ronde tried to catch his breath on the bench.

All day the favored 5–2 Eagles had been trading scores with the 3–4 Panthers. The Eagles, after those first two losses, had been on a roll, winning five games in a row— three of them over highly rated opponents.

Two weeks ago they'd gone over to Martinsville and beat the always-dangerous Colts for the second time in three weeks, 34–17. And last week they'd stomped on the mighty Blue Ridge Bears, 30–10.

On top of that, Ronde reminded himself, the Eagles were the defending district champs. Jefferson hadn't made the play-offs in three years. The Eagles had every reason to be confident about today's contest.

But, as Coach Wheeler liked to say, "That's why they play the games." Statistics meant nothing. The past was the past. Only today mattered. Only *now*. Only this game . . .

The Eagles' quarterback, Cody Hansen, took the snap, and quickly handed off to Tiki. He sliced through the Panthers' defensive line, made a quick cut, and took the ball all the way out to the forty-yard line before he was dragged down from behind.

Ronde let out a whoop and stood up, clapping and pumping his fist. "Yeah!" he shouted. "That's how we do it!" He could feel the momentum shifting like a tidal wave.

On the Eagles' next play, Tiki took another handoff for fifteen yards, crossing into the Panthers' territory.

Tiki looked unstoppable! Ronde and the rest of the defense cheered, and jumped up and down excitedly. But all the while they kept nervously glancing over at the game clock as it ticked down the minutes.

The next play was a pass to Fred Soule for a gain of seven. "Give it to Tiki again!" Ronde shouted, and he wasn't the only one yelling for number 2 to get the ball.

Cody must have heard them, because on the next play he faked a handoff to Tiki, then found him in the flat for a quick completion. It looked like Tiki would be tackled, but he turned the play into a big gain by slipping the grasp of his man. Tiki took off like a rocket, heading for the end zone.

He almost got there too, but the Panthers' free safety, who was playing deep, managed to stop Tiki from notching the score.

It didn't matter, though. Two plays later Tiki dove over the wall of defenders and hit pay dirt. Touchdown, Eagles!

Kicker Adam Costa made the extra point look routine—which it was, for him. Adam had the best record in the league, for the second straight season. And to think, as a seventh grader he'd barely made the team!

Now the Eagles were down by only two, with six minutes still left to play. Adam kicked off to the Panthers, and Ronde, the bird dog on special teams, sped down the field like he'd been shot out of a cannon.

He saw the ball tumble into the arms of number 5—his own number, except on the opposing team. Ronde flew at the ballcarrier, and hit him so hard that the ball came loose!

Too bad it went straight into the arms of another Panthers player.

Still, the Eagles now had their opponents pinned deep in their own territory. If the Panthers wanted to run out the clock, they'd have to either run for a couple of first downs or risk throwing the ball downfield. If they failed either way, they risked stopping the clock and giving the

Eagles time for a desperate comeback drive.

After a running play that went nowhere, the Panthers tried to pass on second down. Ronde bumped his man coming off the line, and the receiver stumbled and fell.

Now the quarterback had to scramble. He spotted a receiver on the other side of the field, and was about to throw to him, when Eagles' defensive end Sam Scarfone tackled him for a sack!

Sam was a ninth grader, but he looked like one of those huge linemen over at the high school. He was a leader on the Eagles, and for a while early in the season he'd sided with Cody Hansen against Coach Wheeler.

But ever since he and Cody had come around, the Eagles had been winning. And now Sam had made a game-changing play.

On third and long, Ronde knew the Panthers would be throwing downfield. He decided not to bump his man this time, but to keep pace with him step for step. He was sure he could do it.

They ran down the field, and Ronde stuck with number 99 like a barnacle on a rock. As they both leapt for the ball, their feet got tangled again—just like before! Hochberg went down as Ronde batted the ball away.

He got up and looked around for the yellow flag, hoping the refs wouldn't make the same bad call as before.

No flag. Thank goodness! Ronde blew out a relieved breath and clapped his hands.

"Interference!" the Panthers' coach yelled, pointing right at Ronde.

The official shook his head and said, "Incidental contact. No penalty."

But the coach didn't see it that way. He called a time-out and walked over to the ref. Ronde couldn't tell what was happening, but before he knew it, Coach Wheeler walked over too.

It seemed like forever until the ref called, "No penalty."

The dismayed receiver trudged over to his own sideline. His coach and teammates came over and gave him pats on the back for support.

Ronde smiled as he lined up to receive the punt. He'd been lucky this time. He knew the call could just as easily have gone the other way. But that was the nature of the game. Sometimes you got the calls, and sometimes you didn't. Either way, though, everyone had to play by the same rules, and the ref's word was the law.

Here came the punt. Ronde grabbed it cleanly, and took off running. The first two Panthers who grabbed at him came up with nothing but air. By the time he was brought down, by the punter, Ronde was at the Panthers' forty-three-yard line!

He looked up at the clock. Only fifty-four seconds left to play! Still, it was plenty of time for the Eagles to make up the two points they needed. A field goal would do it, and Adam was already warming up his golden foot on the sidelines.

On first down Cody took the snap, faked a handoff to Tiki, then rolled out right, looking deep. Fred Soule and Joey Gallagher were both well covered, so Cody looked short and found Tiki at the thirty-five, hitting him right in the numbers. Tiki wheeled around and fought for another seven yards, down to the twenty-eight.

"Wow!" Adam said to Ronde. "Did you see him carry those two mega-thugs with him? Your brother is mad strong!"

"Not as strong as I am," Ronde said coolly.

Adam laughed. "Right. I'm sure. We've got to set up an arm wrestling challenge one of these days."

They turned their eyes back to the field. On second down and three Cody handed off to Tiki, who slashed through the huge hole carved out of the defense by Tiki and Ronde's old pal, center Paco Rivera.

First down, Eagles, at the Panther ten!

Too bad they were out of time-outs, Ronde thought as he jumped up and down in a panic. Coach Wheeler was frantically signaling to Cody to stop the clock. At last, with only six seconds left on the clock, Cody realized what was up and saved the Eagles from disaster by spiking the ball.

"Okay, Costa," Coach Wheeler said, patting Adam on the back. "Get out there and win us this game!"

11

Adam trotted onto the field and got into position. Joey Gallagher, the holder, kneeled down at the seventeen to take the snap. Paco snapped the ball, and Adam drilled the kick right between the uprights, with plenty of leg to spare! The Eagles screamed for joy and ran out onto the field as the final gun sounded. They'd saved their season with a last-second win, 31–30!

"That's about the fourth time in the past season and a half that Adam has saved our bacon," Ronde told Tiki as they high-fived each other. Meanwhile, the rest of the Eagles were carting Adam off the field on their shoulders.

"It's amazing, isn't it?" Tiki said. "Remember when we thought he'd never even make the team?"

"Uh-huh," Ronde said with a laugh. "Worst athlete in the history of our Peewee League—but of course, that was before we found out he could kick!"

CHAPTER TWO

STORM CLOUDS

MRS. BARBER MET TIKI AND RONDE IN THE PARKING lot. She was standing alongside their old brown station wagon and beaming.

"Those are my boys!" she said proudly as they approached, throwing out her arms to give them both a big hug—a "Barber sandwich," she called it. "What a game!"

"I know," Tiki said, shaking his head. "I thought for a while there we were going down."

"For sure," Ronde agreed.

"Not me," said their mom, pursing her lips. "I knew my team was going to pull it out of the fire!" She let out her big hearty laugh, which always made the boys laugh, too. They piled into the old wagon and headed for home.

"What's for dinner?" Ronde asked. "I'm hungry!"

"Starving!" Tiki echoed.

"Well, I'm afraid you boys are just going to have to heat up the mac and cheese I made. I've got to get to work."

"Work?" Tiki said.

"What work?" Ronde asked. "Didn't you just work all day?"

"I did, but I've got a *new* job now. I'm the new store manager at Kroger's."

"Why'd you quit the old job?" Tiki wondered.

"I didn't quit," their mom said, not taking her eyes off the road. "This is a second job. But don't worry—it's only three nights a week."

Tiki was about to open his mouth and ask her why she wanted two jobs, but he caught the look Ronde was giving him.

Tiki knew what that look meant. Times were hard. People were getting fired from their jobs all over town. Houses were up for sale all over the place. Tiki remembered Ms. Colton in social studies class calling it a "recession."

If their mom was taking a second job, on top of her first job at the Virginia Skyline Girl Scout Council, Tiki knew it had to be for a very good reason. He wished he could do something to help out, like babysitting or delivering newspapers.

But with school, and football, and homework, and studying for tests, by the time the weekend rolled around, neither he nor Ronde had much energy left for a job.

They weren't little kids anymore, after all. Tiki remembered back then, when they played football out in the street nonstop, from morning till night. Still, he couldn't just let his mom do all that work without offering to help, could he?

"Mom," he said, "I was thinking, maybe I could get a paper route. You know, go around on my bike before school and—"

She cut him off with a wave of her hand. "If I ever need you boys to help, I'll let you know, all right? But I sure do hope that day never comes." Tiki could tell she meant it.

"Why are you sad, Mom?" Tiki asked her.

"I'm just so proud of you boys," she said. "Don't you worry about me, Tiki and Ronde. Hard work never hurt anybody. I'll take care of putting food on the table. You boys just keep bringing home those good grades."

"What good grades?" Tiki asked, suddenly forgetting all his worries about money.

"Did our report cards come in the mail?" Ronde asked, leaning forward excitedly in the backseat.

"They sure did," Mrs. Barber said, beaming.

"Mom, did you open them?" Tiki moaned. He had worked hard, but he hadn't seen his exam grades, and science was hard. He almost hadn't even finished the test!

"Well, the envelopes weren't sealed," she said, chuckling. "Besides, they were addressed to me."

She pulled the car to the curb in front of their house. "Don't worry, boys. You did just fine. Now, out you go.

I'll be back around eleven. You'd best be asleep, both of you. I'll come in and kiss you good night."

The boys got out of the car and watched as it disappeared around the corner at the end of the street.

Tiki shook his head. He and Ronde had the best mom in the whole world, no doubt about it. And even if it meant going blind from too much studying, he was going to bring home all As for her for the rest of the school year—no, for the rest of his life!

He turned to go inside, and saw the look on his brother's face. Tiki knew Ronde was thinking right along with him. Funny how they thought as much alike as they looked.

Tiki wondered if it would always be that way. It wasn't as true now as it used to be when they were little kids, way back in sixth grade.

"I'm hungry," Ronde said, breaking the spell. "Let's eat!"

They ran inside and checked out their grades while the mac and cheese heated up in the oven.

"I got an A in Biology," Tiki said.

"So what's new?" Ronde cracked. "You always get As in science."

"Yeah, what'd *you* get, big shot?"

"B plus."

"Ha!"

"But I got an A *plus* in math—and that's harder than biology."

"No, it's not. That's totally bogus!" Tiki didn't want to admit he'd gotten only an A in math.

"You know," Tiki said, "if I don't make the NFL someday, I think I might become a scientist. Maybe even an astronaut, so I could check out if there's life on Mars."

"You sure do have your head in the clouds," Ronde cracked, giggling. "I wouldn't be surprised if you were from another planet."

"Oh yeah, smart guy? How'd *you* do in history?"

"Never mind. I got as many As as you did, I bet."

"No way!"

"Yes way."

They counted. Tiki had one more A than Ronde. "So what?" Ronde said, shrugging it off. "I'm not gonna be an astronaut. While you're up on Mars, I'll be down here in the Super Bowl, waving up to you."

This went on until the smell from the oven told them their food was ready to eat. That put an end to the argument, at least for the moment.

"Man!" Ronde said, rubbing his belly and staring at his empty plate. "That was goo-oood!"

"Mom is an awesome cook, isn't she?" Tiki said, taking the plates to the sink and rinsing them off. "Come on, lazybones. Help me with these dishes. Let's leave her a clean sink to come home to."

They did the dishes, and soon the conversation got

back to the big game. "I thought Coach was going to give you the game ball," Ronde said.

"Nah," Tiki said, smiling. "Adam deserved it. Can you see anybody else putting that ball between the uprights under all that pressure?"

"He's our team MVP so far this season," Ronde agreed. "Hands down. Hey, let's call and give him noise about it, just for laughs!"

That sounded like a good idea to Tiki. They'd joke around and hash over the game together. Adam was the funniest kid they knew. Half the time, he was cracking hilarious jokes, and the other half, he had no idea he was being funny. Either way, he was a great guy. They'd all been friends since way back in Peewee League.

Adam had never been much of an athlete. It was amazing he'd made the football team at all. Who would have thought he'd turn out to be such a good kicker?

It was amazing, Tiki thought, how many hidden talents people had. His mom, for instance—she'd stopped a polluting factory from being built in the neighborhood, single-handed! Well, almost. But he'd never known before then that she was such a great leader.

Adam's mother answered the phone—and to Tiki's surprise she didn't sound too happy. "Adam's in his room," she said. "And he's not coming down. You'll have to see him tomorrow in school."

Tiki hung up, puzzled. Ronde came back in from

the living room, where he'd been listening on the other extension. "What was that all about?" he asked.

Tiki shrugged. "I have no clue. But it sure is weird."

"She sounded mad," Ronde said. "You'd think she'd be proud of Adam, after he won the big game like that."

"She wasn't at the game," Tiki reminded Ronde. "She never is."

"Does she work?"

Tiki shook his head. "Nah. She doesn't like sports, remember?"

"Oh, that's right," Ronde said. "Oh, well. We can tease Adam about that, too, huh?"

"Sure thing," Tiki said, laughing even though he didn't think it was so funny.

They did their homework and went to bed, but Tiki had trouble sleeping. Across the room he could hear Ronde tossing and turning too.

The house was too quiet without their mom moving around downstairs, watching TV or cooking or talking on the phone. Every little creak and groan of the old wooden beams made Tiki's eyes pop open.

But it wasn't fear that was keeping him awake. A little flame of worry was burning inside him. Something was going on at Adam's house, he was sure—and whatever it was, it wasn't good.

Nothing keeps a person awake more than not knowing the answer to a mystery, Tiki thought.

19

From across the room he heard Ronde sigh.

Twins think alike, he told himself.

"Honor roll, dude!" Tiki bragged, holding up his report card for the whole lunch table to see.

"Gimme that!" said Paco. "This is garbage, man. You stole a blank report card from the office and typed in the grades yourself!"

Tiki laughed and shook his head. He and wide receiver Joey Gallagher had the highest grades at the table, with Ronde only slightly behind. Most of the kids had a lot of Bs and Cs, with a few Ds sprinkled in here and there. Those Ds might be good for laughs now, but they were a real pain when you had to explain them to your parents.

"Hey, it's only midterms," Cody Hansen pointed out. "By the time the term ends I'll have a higher average than any of you guys. You'll see."

Cody, the team's quarterback, was getting less annoying. He was no longer unbearable as he'd been back in September when the term and the season had started. But he still had a little of the old braggart in him. "When it's time for finals, football season'll be over, and there'll be more time to study."

"Not if we make it to the state finals, dude," Fred Soule said. Fred was the team's other wide receiver. He and Joey were both ninth graders, as was Cody.

"True," Cody said. "And we *will* get there—for *sure.*"

The Eagles' confidence was sky-high at the moment. Six straight wins will do that for a team.

It was a huge change from earlier in the season, when Cody just couldn't get in sync with the rest of them, and nobody could figure out which way the new coach was leading them.

But ever since they'd started working together, and really getting behind Coach Wheeler's system, they'd been total world-beaters. They hadn't lost a single game since.

"Hey, let's not get over-confident," Ronde said, putting up a hand. "There are still a few games left before we can say we're in the play-offs. And you know if we lose even one of those games, the teams ahead of us have to lose, or else we're out of it."

"Don't sweat it," Cody said with a smirk. "We're *not* losing another game, Barber. With Costa's leg on our side, we're golden, right?"

They all laughed. It was funny that the shortest, skinniest, nerdiest kid on the team was actually their most valuable player.

"Say, where *is* Adam, anyway?" Paco wondered. "He *never* misses lunch. He eats more than any of us."

Again, everyone laughed.

"Didn't he beat you in an eating contest once?" Tiki reminded Paco.

"The kid is a total animal," Paco said with a mock shiver. "He's a freak. I can't believe somebody that thin can pack in so many doughnuts."

"Was he absent today or something?" Ronde wondered.

"He'd better not be sick," said Paco. "We need him this week against the Mountaineers."

"Hey," said Cody. "He's playing, okay? As long as his leg's not broken, who cares if he sneezes all over the locker room?"

"Eeeeuw!" everyone groaned. "Gross!"

"No, man," said Sam Scarfone. "He's not sick. I saw him going into the office on my way down here."

"Oh," Ronde said. "Well, in that case, maybe he went to see the nurse."

"Not *that* office, dude," Sam said. "The principal's office."

There was a sudden silence at the table. Everyone's eyes went wide. "What'd he do, beat some kid up?" Paco joked.

Everyone laughed nervously. Tiki knew it wouldn't be so funny if Adam was in real trouble.

But he can't be! he told himself. Adam never got into trouble. He wasn't the kind of kid who had behavior problems.

Tiki looked over at Ronde, who looked as queasy as Tiki felt. Something was definitely up with Adam. They'd just have to wait till practice to find out *what*.

• • •

"*That's* what I'm talking about!" Coach Wheeler shouted, clapping his hands and smiling as the team executed yet another play perfectly.

Too bad it isn't a game, Tiki thought as he took his position behind Cody for the next play. *We've never played this well before, even in practice!*

They were running all their set plays today, with only light contact—no real hitting. Tiki looked around for Adam. He wanted to ask him why his mom had been mad, and why he hadn't shown up for lunch. But Adam was nowhere to be found.

Tiki figured he must have gotten sick. Adam never missed a football practice otherwise. Tiki sure hoped it was nothing serious. They were going to need him against the Mountaineers on Thursday.

"Ohio State, on four," Coach Wheeler called the play in, then watched as the Eagles' offense went through its paces like a finely tuned machine. "You guys come out like this on Thursday, and we're gonna get ourselves another big win!" he shouted.

Ohio State was a quick screen pass for Tiki. He had been working on his moves for this play because it involved a certain amount of acting. Tiki had to make it seem like he was really blocking the rusher, even though he was letting him get through to Cody on purpose.

Then Tiki had to turn on a dime, just as the pass was

23

being floated toward him. If it worked like it was supposed to, Ohio State was designed to pick up anywhere from five to ten yards. But the way Tiki could dodge and deke in the open field, it might also result in a touchdown.

Tiki ran the play to perfection. Then he turned to make sure that Coach Wheeler had been watching. He was disappointed to see that the coach hadn't been looking at all! Instead he was deep in conversation with Mrs. Franklin, the assistant principal.

What's she doing out here? Tiki wondered. If there was a problem with one of Mr. Wheeler's students, why didn't she wait and talk to him when he was in the office, or in the teachers' lounge? Why did she have to interrupt football practice? Didn't she realize how important it was that the coach concentrate on his team?

Wheeler stood with his arms folded across his chest. He looked very serious, with that eagle's frown of his. He nodded every now and then as Mrs. Franklin spoke. Then he would look down at the ground, scuffing it with his shoe.

Tiki got a funny feeling in his stomach. What were they talking about? Not *him*, he hoped!

No, it couldn't be about him. His grades were good— near the top of his class. And Ronde's were too.

Still, Mrs. Franklin being there was not a good sign. She was a nice lady, kind of, but she almost always brought bad news.

24

"Hey, Coach!" Cody yelled, cupping his hands in front of his mouth. "What next?"

Coach Wheeler looked up, startled, like he'd been brought back down to Earth. "Um, Georgia Tech. And look sharp. Let's go!"

He clapped his hands a couple of times, and the boys lined up to run the play. Tiki glanced back over his shoulder as Cody called for the snap. Coach Wheeler wasn't even looking. He and Mrs. Franklin were deep in their own little world.

The play went perfectly—every play that day went better than ever before. But as good as that made Tiki feel, it upset him that Coach had missed so much of it.

After practice, when they had showered, gotten back into their street clothes, and were about to leave for home, Coach Wheeler called for their attention. "Listen up, you guys."

Something about the tone of his voice made everyone stop what they were doing. The room was deathly quiet.

"Some of you may have noticed that Adam Costa wasn't at practice today," he said.

A low murmur made its way around the room. A few of the players nodded their heads.

"Mrs. Franklin has informed me that Adam has been placed on academic probation."

A gasp went up from the players.

"*What?*" Cody said.

"Academic probation," the coach repeated. "It's serious business."

"Wow," Cody said, shaking his head. "That really stinks for him."

"He'll have to do some makeup work," Coach Wheeler continued. "Hopefully he'll pass next go-round. But here's the really bad news: Until he passes his makeup tests in both subjects, school rules say he's barred from all extracurricular activities. In other words, until Costa's grades improve, *no more football.*"

CHAPTER THREE
REACHING OUT

A LOUD MOAN OF PROTEST WENT UP FROM THE players. "Noooooo!" "What?" "No way!"

Mr. Wheeler held up his hands to quiet them, but it took a while for the ruckus to die down.

"I'm sorry, guys," he said. "I don't like it any more than you do. But those are the rules, and there's nothing we can do about it but play our hearts out, try to win on Thursday, and hope that Adam aces his makeup tests and gets back with the team—*soon*."

In the quiet locker room the full meaning of what had happened now began to sink in. "Why is Mrs. Franklin doing this to us?" Paco complained. "What did *we* do wrong?"

"Nothing," Mr. Wheeler replied. "Nothing at all. Not one little thing. Still . . ."

"How could she do this to us?" Joey protested. "Doesn't she realize Adam's been our MVP this season?"

"I don't know about *that*," said Cody, who had always thought of *himself* as the team's most valuable player.

Cody was the quarterback, so he had a point, sort

of—but even *Cody* would have had to admit that Adam was the hardest Eagle to replace. After all, there was a backup quarterback—Manny Alvaro—but there was no backup kicker.

On top of that, Adam was both their placekicker and their punter! They depended on his leg for everything from field goals to extra points to kickoffs to punts!

"I can't believe Mrs. Franklin would sabotage her own school," said Sam Scarfone, slamming his meaty hand on a locker door.

"Man, is she for real?" Paco said.

"Don't blame Mrs. Franklin," Coach Wheeler warned. "She doesn't like it either. But it's her job to enforce the school rules."

"Well, who decides what the school rules are?" Fred Soule asked. "Nobody here ever got to vote on them."

"Look," the coach said, "at the end of the day, it's the principal who makes the rules. That's the way it is. You all knew the rules about academic probation from day one, and we all have to live by them, Adam included."

"It still stinks," Cody said.

"Yeah," Sam agreed. "I mean, who takes any of that stuff seriously?"

Coach Wheeler shrugged. "Like it or not, you'd better take it seriously. That's how it is in any school, guys. Hidden Valley's no different."

Ronde liked Dr. Anand, the principal. When she'd

picked Coach Wheeler to take over the Eagles after Coach Spangler had left the team, nobody had thought it was a good idea. But it had turned out pretty well so far. In spite of all their troubles, the Eagles still had a shot at making the play-offs.

No, wait—that was when they still had Adam.

Without him, as far as Ronde could see, their chances for a championship were just about zero.

"I don't understand," he said aloud. "How could this happen to us?"

"Yeah, just when everything was going perfect," Bill Reeves added.

"We were headed for the play-offs for sure," Fred Soule chimed in. "Now? Forget it."

"Hey, it's not *that* bad," Cody objected. "I mean, *I'm* still here."

Ronde shook his head and rolled his eyes. Cody sure did have a high opinion of himself.

"We're *all* still here," Tiki said.

"Yeah, all except our team MVP," Paco pointed out. "Without him who's gonna kick all those field goals and extra points? And who's gonna nail the other team deep in their own end?"

Suddenly it hit Ronde—Paco was right! "Hey, Coach?"

"Yes?"

"Who *is* going to do the kicking on Thursday?"

29

Coach Wheeler sighed. "I'm going to try some of you out at tomorrow's practice. Anyone who thinks he might be good at it, or wants to learn, I'll be looking for volunteers."

Ronde blew out a breath. Volunteering to be Adam Costa's replacement was asking for a world of pressure.

"Meanwhile," Coach Wheeler said, "let's try to stay optimistic. After all, we're on a six-game winning streak, right? If you all do your jobs—and, by the way, that includes keeping your *own* grades up—we'll get through this and be fine in the end."

Ronde took a look around the locker room. In spite of Coach Wheeler's upbeat words, there was not a one of them who looked the least bit optimistic about things turning out "fine in the end."

"Remember when Adam hit that field goal from the twenty-eight-yard line?" Tiki said as they headed for the late bus that would take them home.

"Yeah, man," Ronde said, smiling in spite of his dark mood. Kicking from the twenty-eight meant it was a twenty-eight-yard field goal—incredibly long for junior high. "And he's such a skinny kid too. And his punts are even longer. He can kick it almost fifty yards—more, if he gets a good bounce."

"We're sunk if he doesn't come back," Tiki said.

"Dude, he's *not* coming back," Ronde said. "Not this week, anyway. Remember what Coach said?"

Tiki shook his head. "I don't care what *anybody* says. We've got to get Adam back, before it's too late and our season goes down the drain!"

Ronde agreed. They had to do something, all right—but what?

It was hard to concentrate on homework that night. Ronde kept putting his pencil down and rubbing his eyes. He pressed so hard that he saw colors and lights when he closed them.

But it didn't help. The same old homework was still staring up at him, waiting to be finished.

Was this how Adam felt *all the time*? Ronde knew Adam wasn't the best student, but he'd never actually *failed* a class before.

Maybe Mrs. Franklin was right. Maybe all the time Adam was spending at football practice *was* hurting his grades.

He remembered what Tiki had said: *We've got to get Adam back!*

"Maybe we should call Adam," Ronde suggested.

Tiki looked up from the other side of the kitchen table, where he had his homework spread in front of him. "Good idea," he said.

Ronde started to get up, but he realized that Tiki wasn't moving. "*You* call him, Tiki," he said, sitting back down.

31

"*Me*? Why me? It was *your* idea!"

"You know you were thinking of it too."

"So what if I was? You're the one who said it out loud!"

"What are you, chicken?"

"*Me? You're* the one who's chicken!"

"Am not!"

"Are too!"

"Am not!"

"Are too!"

Ronde slammed his hand down on his textbook. "All right, all right!"

But he didn't get up to make the call. "You know," he said after a long pause, "Adam might not want to hear from anybody right now. He might not want to talk about it at all."

Tiki considered this. "Yeah, you know, you may be right. He's probably so embarrassed about failing his midterms . . ."

"And letting the team down . . ."

"Exactly!"

"Calling him about it might feel like we were rubbing it in."

"Piling on! You're right."

"We'd better wait till he has a chance to get over it."

"You think?"

"Definitely. Don't you?"

"I guess," Tiki said, sighing. "Poor Adam."

"I know. It really, really stinks," Ronde agreed.

They both went back to doing their homework. But Ronde felt worse than ever, and he was sure Tiki did too.

All that baloney about Adam feeling embarrassed— he and Tiki both knew it was the two of *them* who were nervous—about *calling*. What if they said the wrong thing, and Adam started to cry or something? That would only make a bad situation worse!

"So . . . you're not gonna call him?" Ronde asked.

"Why are you asking *me*?" Tiki said. "Didn't we just agree it would be a bad idea?"

"Well, yeah, but . . ."

Just then they heard the front door open, and their mom came into the house.

"Besides," Tiki added, "I've got a history quiz Thursday."

"Don't look at me," Ronde shot back. "I've got an English quiz."

"So what? You're good at English!"

"So? You're good at history!"

"What are you two arguing about now?" Mrs. Barber asked, dropping her purse onto the table right between them.

The purse was almost as big as a suitcase. It was jam-packed full of stuff too. It made a big thump when it hit the table.

"Nothing, Mom," Ronde said, glaring at Tiki.

"Don't give me 'nothing,' Ronde," she warned. "Tell me what's going on."

"Sorry, Mom," he said. "I didn't mean it that way. It's just . . . too awful to talk about."

"*Really?*" she said, taking a seat between them at the table. "In that case you'd better give me the *whole story, right now.*"

Ronde and Tiki looked at each other, and sank down in their chairs. When their mom laid down the law, they both knew they'd best listen.

"*You* tell her," Tiki said.

"*Me? You* tell her!"

"Now, don't start in on *that* again," said Mrs. Barber. "Ronde, you start. Then, Tiki, you fill in whatever he left out."

"Yes, Mom," said Tiki.

"Yes, Mom," said Ronde.

When she'd heard the whole story, Mrs. Barber's brow wrinkled in concern. "That poor boy. Think how awful he must feel. To fail in *two subjects*, and to be taken off the team, too!"

"I know," said Tiki. "It's so *unfair!*"

"No, it's not unfair," said Mrs. Barber. "If the school has a rule, there's usually a good reason for it."

"Sure," Ronde said, sulking. "To punish the whole team."

"Ronde!"

"It's true, Mom!" Tiki chimed in. "Just because Adam messed up, why do we *all* have to suffer? We didn't do anything wrong."

"No, you didn't," she agreed. "But let me ask you this—do you think a school should allow its students to fail?"

Tiki and Ronde looked at each other glumly.

"Well?"

"No, ma'am," they both said.

She got up. "I'm glad to see you're both doing your homework. I know that if either of my boys ever failed a course, I'd want your school to take it seriously."

"But what about the rest of the team?" Tiki protested.

"Yeah, what about us?" Ronde echoed.

Their mom shrugged. "Maybe instead of moping around you ought to think about what you can do to get Adam back on the team."

"Huh?"

"Like what?" Tiki asked.

Mrs. Barber smiled and headed for the stairs. "Oh, I don't know. But you're smart boys. I know you'll come up with something. Remember, where there's a will there's a way."

After she left, the boys looked at each other. "Well, I'm stumped," said Ronde. "You got any bright ideas?"

To Ronde's surprise Tiki had that look in his eye that said he *did* have one.

35

"Ronde, Adam's failing in math and biology, right?"

"Yeah. So?"

"Well, I'm good at biology. And you got an A in math, didn't you?"

"A plus. But—"

"Why don't we call Adam up and offer to help him study for his makeup tests?"

Ronde thought about this for a moment. "I don't know," he said. "I've never tutored anybody before . . ."

"So what?" Tiki said. "There's a first time for everything, right?"

"I guess . . . but what if we offer and Adam gets embarrassed about it?"

"Hey, man, let's not worry about that. He can always say no."

"Mmmm . . . I don't know . . ."

"Look, we can just say we called to see how he was doing, and then . . . you know, kind of like we just thought of it right then?"

"Okay," Ronde finally agreed. He went over to the phone, removed it from the hook, and handed it to Tiki. "Go on. Take it."

"Why me?" he asked.

"What do you mean, why you? It was your idea!"

"Yeah, but you're the oldest."

"By seven minutes!" Ronde shot back.

"Come on, Ronde!"

Ronde held the phone out to Tiki, not budging.

"Okay," Tiki said, "you dial. I'll go into the living room and pick up the extension. That way we *both* make the call, *together*."

Ronde frowned, but relented. "Okay. Go on in there, then."

"Start dialing first."

"Look, dude, why don't we wait till tomorrow. Maybe we'll run into him at school or something. Maybe by then somebody else will—"

"Ronde, we're Adam's best friends on the team. If calling is too embarrassing for us, you *know* nobody else is going to do it."

"All right, all right." Ronde punched in the phone number while Tiki went into the living room to listen in on the extension.

"Yes?" Mrs. Costa's voice sounded pained—or was that just Ronde's imagination?

"Um, this is Ronde Barber?"

"Yes?"

"Could I . . . Um, could I speak to Adam, please?"

A sigh. "Sure. Just hang on a minute. I have to go get him. He's in his room."

Ronde could hear the phone being put down, then silence.

"Man," Ronde said, "seems like he's always up in his room."

"I know," Tiki replied on the extension. "And his mom is always yelling at him too."

Ronde let out a chuckle, remembering how Adam liked to do his impression of his parents yelling at him. It had been funny at the time, but now Ronde realized it might not be so funny in real life.

He heard the phone being picked up, dropped to the floor, and then picked up again. "Hello? Sorry. Hello?" came Adam's voice.

"Hey, dude," Ronde said. "It's me."

"And me too," Tiki added.

"Hi, guys!" Adam said. "Man, am I ever glad you called."

"You are?" Ronde said.

"Totally! I thought nobody was ever going to talk to me again, after the way I let the whole team down."

"Now, don't say that—," Ronde began.

"You didn't let anybody down, except maybe yourself," Tiki assured him.

"You mean it?"

Well, not really, thought Ronde. He and Tiki had certainly had their moments of blaming Adam. After all, if he'd studied a little harder, maybe none of this would have happened.

Still, he could tell that Adam was hurting, and neither he nor Tiki had the heart to hurt his feelings any further.

"Everybody's in your corner, dude," Ronde assured him.

"Definitely," Tiki agreed. "It's so unfair, what they're doing to you!"

"To all of us!" Ronde added.

Ronde could hear a tremble in Adam's voice when he said, "I'm really sorry, guys. Tell everyone, okay? I didn't mean to mess up so bad. I don't know how I failed those tests. I was like, 'Did we really go over this in class?' I swear, it was like reading *Chinese*. I couldn't even figure out what some of the *questions* were, let alone the answers!"

"Hey, man," Tiki said, "don't worry about letting the team down, okay? We'll find a way to keep winning somehow. You just work hard, pass those tests, and get back quick."

"Hey, you know what?" said Ronde, remembering his mom's words. "Tiki and I sometimes study together. Maybe we could get together and help you study for your makeup exams?"

"Wow, that's really amazing of you guys to offer," said Adam, sniffing again. "But it's okay. They've already lined me up with a tutor. Some ninth grader."

"What's his name?" Tiki asked. "Anybody we know?"

"It's not a him; it's a her. Melody somebody."

"Melody Burghammer? Isn't she on the chess team?" Ronde asked.

"And the computer team, and the debating team, and the science olympiad—and she plays *piano*, too. I figure if *she* can't help me, I'm *really* in trouble."

That was Adam, thought Ronde. Always with the jokes, no matter how bad the reality was.

"Anyway, I guess I'm set with tutoring, but thanks for the offer anyway."

"So, when do you think you'll be back with the team?" Ronde asked. It was the question on everyone's mind, not just his and Tiki's.

There was a long pause. "Um . . . I don't really know," said Adam. "I've got my first tutoring session tomorrow—"

"What about Thursday's game?" Tiki broke in. "Can you take your makeup tests by then?"

"Dude," said Adam, "that's the day after tomorrow."

"I know, but—"

"Sorry," said Adam, heaving a huge sigh. "I know I'm not smart."

"Hey! You're not *stupid*," Ronde told him.

"That's right. If you study hard, you can get those grades up," added Tiki.

"Thanks, but there's no way I'll be back in time for the Mountaineers game," Adam said sadly. "Maybe for the week after."

"MAYBE?"

"Hey, it's two subjects, not one—and they have to get

the teachers to stay after school to proctor me when I take the retests, so it has to be on certain days. Anyway, it's gonna take me a while to get all those factoids through my thick skull."

Ronde smiled. It was good to hear that Adam still had his sense of humor.

"Meanwhile," said Adam, "who's gonna be our kicker on Thursday?"

There was a long, long silence.

Who *was* going to kick for the Eagles on Thursday?

It was the million-dollar question. And so far *nobody* had any answers.

CHAPTER FOUR

THE SEARCH FOR THE GOLDEN FOOT

BY THE TIME PRACTICE ROLLED AROUND ON Wednesday, a lot of the team members had run into Adam and gotten the lowdown on his situation. Five minutes into drills, everyone on the Eagles knew how things stood.

They simply had to forget about Adam for now and try to win without him.

It's possible, Tiki told himself. The Eagles were on a six-game winning streak, after all. Besides, it wasn't like the Mountaineers were unbeatable. They had a losing record of 3–5, so under normal conditions the 6–2 Eagles would have been favored.

But without a kicker?

When Coach Wheeler blew his whistle at the end of drills, it usually meant it was time to run plays, and then scrimmage. Today was different.

"Boys," he said, "I'm going to send most of you over to the home end of the field, to work with Coach Ontkos and Coach Pellugi. I'm going to stay at this end, to try to find some potential replacements for Costa. So first of all,

42

raise your hands—is there anybody here who thinks he can kick?"

Tiki looked around. Every single kid's hand stayed down at his side. Nobody—nobody wanted to try to fill Adam's golden shoes.

When he thought about it, Tiki wasn't surprised. Adam was a hard act to follow—and whoever became his replacement would be under a huge magnifying glass.

Sure, if the new kicker came through, he would be a hero to the whole school, let alone the team. But if he failed . . .

Not me, Tiki thought. *Somebody else can have that chance, and I wish them all the luck.*

At that very moment Coach Wheeler tapped him on the shoulder. "Barber," he said, "I want you to try out."

"Me?"

"Sure, why not. Just give it a try, okay?"

Tiki hesitated. "Uh . . ."

"Don't worry. You can still start at running back."

"Yeah, but—" Tiki knew he had to think fast if he wanted to get out of this. "How about Ronde?"

Coach Wheeler shook his head. "Nope. Can't spare him. How's he going to kick and be on the kickoff and punt teams' rush at the same time? You know he's always the first one to hit the returner."

Tiki gave up trying to get out of it. He stayed with Coach Wheeler and five other players—including Joey

Gallagher, who was the holder, and Paco, the long snapper. And since neither of those guys was trying out . . .

Yikes! It suddenly hit Tiki that he had a one in three chance of being picked!

First to try his luck was Fred Soule. Fred, the team's best wide receiver, was tall and thin, with big hands that were perfect for reeling in long passes. But Fred's feet, which were also big, were not so talented. Fred's kicks were knuckleballs that twisted left, right, and straight into the ground.

Next up was John Berra, Tiki's fellow running back. Unlike Tiki, John was built thick and solid. He was more of a fullback type—a bull who ran straight ahead into the line, dragging defenders down the field with him.

His kicks were all line drives. Some of them went a long way, but others hit the ground and bounced straight backward. He just didn't seem to have the flexibility to get under the ball and give it some lift. "Man, I really stink at this," John said. "Coach, can I go now?"

Coach Wheeler shook his head. "So far you're the best we've got, I'm afraid." He turned to Tiki. "Your turn, Barber. Let's see what *you* can do."

Tiki's first try at a punt was a complete whiff—he totally missed the ball, and went tumbling to the ground in a backward somersault. Everyone laughed, and even Tiki had to chuckle at his own clumsiness. "Yeah, baby!" he said. "That's what I'm talking about!"

On his second try he shanked it off the side of his foot. But after that his punts started to improve. Some were end-over-end, but others were perfect spirals. They went a good distance, but, just as important, they were straight, and they stayed in the air long enough to let the rushers get downfield and tackle the returner.

"Hmm," said Coach Wheeler, taking notes. "Not bad, Barber. Not bad at all, if you don't count the first few."

Tiki winced. Had his punting really been better than Fred's or John's? *He* didn't think so—but he had to admit he was prejudiced against himself, because no way did he want this job.

"Okay, let's try some placekicking, guys," said Coach Wheeler. "Joey, Paco—take your positions."

Paco got into his crouch, gripping the ball so he could make the long snap. Joey kneeled down at the fifteen yard line, ready to take the snap.

"Barber, you go first this time," said Coach Wheeler.

Tiki looked down at Joey, who was looking back up at him from his crouch.

"Don't be nervous," Joey told him. "There's nothing to it. Piece of cake."

"Yeah, right," Tiki said. "Big enough piece to choke on."

They laughed, and Tiki felt his mood lighten. His first kick was a beauty—straight down the field and through the middle of the uprights.

"Hey, hey, hey!" said Coach Wheeler, breaking into a relieved smile. "I think we might have found something here!"

"No, no, no," Tiki said, waving his hands. "That was just a lucky kick."

His next attempt was wide right, but at least it had the height and distance. He kicked several more, and half of them were actually *good*, as in *three points* good.

John and Fred followed, but they needn't have bothered. From that moment on Tiki could tell by the coach's face that he'd made up his mind.

"Well, Tiki," he said, putting an arm around his shoulders when the tryouts were done. "Until further notice, you're the man."

"Hey, congratulations," John said, patting Tiki on the back.

"Yeah, nice going, Tiki," Fred said, giving him five.

Tiki thanked them, but his heart wasn't in it.

When they got back to the home end of the field, Coach Wheeler blew his whistle. "Okay, team, Tiki's our kicker for the Mountaineers game."

A cheer went up from the players, but Tiki could tell they weren't really happy about it. Neither was he.

"I'm going to take some time now to put in a couple of two-point conversion plays, just in case things don't go well," the coach went on. "I have a feeling we're going to need them."

The others all laughed. But when Tiki heard those words, his heart sank from his chest right down to his shoes.

To think—just a few days ago he'd been really looking forward to this game against the Mountaineers. Now he was dreading it like the plague.

All day Thursday, Tiki could not concentrate in class. He managed to get it together for his history quiz pretty well—at least he hoped so. If he failed, it might be the first step on the way to Adam-land. In other words, *no football*.

He couldn't decide which was worse—no football or having to be the Eagles' kicker in Adam's place. In the end he figured he might as well play. After all, whatever points he gave away as the kicker, he could always get back with a big running game.

It seemed to him that the Eagles' chances were better with him playing than without. But who knew what could happen? He might blow the whole game by muffing kicks!

It was a nightmare. In fact, he'd had a nightmare about it the night before. In his dream the football grew big teeth and opened its jaws wide to swallow his foot just as he was about to kick a field goal! He woke up yelling, grabbing his foot—which, thank goodness, was still there after all.

Now, as the bell rang to signal the end of the school day, Tiki knew he had to suck up his fears and do what had to be done. All he could do was cross his fingers and trust to luck—and to his football instincts, of course.

All the other Eagles encouraged him before the game, pumping him up as they rode the team bus across town to East Side Junior High.

Their support made Tiki feel better—so much better that when the Eagles won the coin toss and elected to receive, he almost wished they'd lost it, so he could kick off right away and get over his case of the jitters.

Ronde ran the kickoff back twenty yards, and the Eagles started their first drive in good field position, at their own forty-three yard line.

Tiki strapped on his helmet and trotted onto the field along with Cody, Fred, Joey, John, Paco, and the rest of the Eagles' offense. They huddled up, and everyone put their hands together, one on top of the other.

"Let's go, Eagles!" Cody shouted, and they all let out a cheer. Tiki lined up for the first play, glad to be in his familiar place at running back. He tried to force all thoughts of kicking out of his head, at least for the moment.

The first play was a handoff. Tiki took the ball, dodged left, then right, waiting for the hole to open in the line. But it never did. The Mountaineers might not have been a winning team, but they sure were beefy on the defensive line. It was going to be a tough day to run, Tiki realized.

On second down Coach called an option pass for Cody. The quarterback took the snap, rolled to his right, and tossed it long for Joey Gallagher. But the pass was underthrown. It hit the defender right in the helmet.

Now it was third down, and nine to go. Another passing down. And if Cody couldn't connect with any of his receivers, it would be time for Tiki to punt!

Tiki lined up for the play. He tried to swallow, but his throat was dry, and he could hear his breath rushing loudly in his ears.

His job was to block for Cody, intercepting any blitzing defensive backs or linebackers that broke through the pocket. But his breathing was echoing so loudly that he couldn't hear the signals Cody was calling!

The first thing he knew, everyone was launching into the play, while he was still in his three-point stance. Before he even knew what was happening, the Mountaineers cornerback was bowling him over backward, on his way to a vicious blindside sack of Cody!

Tiki groaned and grabbed his helmet with both hands. "That's okay, Barber," Cody said, getting up, shaking it off, and slapping Tiki on the shoulder. "We'll get 'em next series."

"My bad," Tiki said, tapping himself on the chest and sighing in frustration. He knew he was lucky that Cody had changed his way of thinking over the course of the season. In the bad old days, a few weeks back, he would have bitten Tiki's head off for missing that block!

But why, Tiki wondered, hadn't he been able to keep his mind in the moment? He'd certainly tried to concentrate—but he'd *failed*! And as a result he'd made *sure* he'd have to punt.

Tiki stood back there, waiting for the long snap from Paco. "Just like yesterday, when I was trying out," Tiki told himself in a low voice. "No different. Same story. No problem. No—"

Again he'd been lost in his own thoughts, and now here came the snap, zipping straight at him!

Tiki managed to catch the ball, but instinctively he caught it like a receiver and drew it into his chest, instead of holding it out in front of him so he could kick it!

He caught himself in a fraction of a second and corrected his mistake, with the monstrous Mountaineers rushers coming at him, their hands held high and screaming at the top of their lungs.

THUNK! Tiki managed—barely—to get the kick away. But it was high and end-over-end, a short kick that bounced straight back toward them. A pile of players dove onto it and downed it at the Eagles' forty-nine yard line.

The end result? *A seven yard punt!*

Tiki felt the blood rush to his face and his eyes fill with tears. He blinked them back, heading for the sideline with his helmet still strapped on to help hide his face.

"Don't worry about it, Tiki," Coach Wheeler called to him as he reached the bench. "First one's always tough. Just try to relax out there."

Tiki nodded, but didn't say anything. The lump in his throat was so big, he couldn't have spoken even if he'd wanted to.

Tiki sat there while the Eagles went on defense. None of his teammates looked him in the eye, or sat near him, or even tried to talk to him.

Tiki knew what they were thinking. They weren't mad or anything. No, not at all. They pitied him. They knew he hadn't asked to be the kicker, and that it wasn't his fault that he stunk at it.

No, if they were mad at anyone, it was Adam—or better yet, the school officials. They were the ones responsible, not him. Not him—

A roar went up from the crowd. Tiki stood up and tried to see what was going on. "What happened?" he asked Paco, who was standing next to him, yelling his head off and pumping his fists.

"Dude, what are you, sleeping? Your brother just picked off a screen pass and ran it all the way for a touchdown!"

"Wa-hoo!" Tiki yelled, jumping up and down now himself. Good old Ronde, picking his brother up when he was down!

And then he realized—*it was time for the extra point!*

Tiki looked pleadingly at Coach Wheeler, hoping he would call for the two-point conversion play he'd practiced with the team the day before.

But the coach just looked back at Tiki, clapping his hands. "Get out there and split those uprights, Barber!"

Tiki swallowed hard, and tried to make his heart slow down as he jogged slowly, reluctantly back onto the field.

"Breathe," he told himself, blowing out gusts of air as he focused on Joey's hands, which were poised to receive the snap.

"Hut!" he called out.

Tiki saw the ball arrive in Joey's hands. He saw Joey place the ball perfectly on the turf, waiting for Tiki to launch the kick.

Tiki took one step, then another, and let his foot swing down at the ball and through. He looked up to see where it went—and watched as the ball flew low, hit the crossbar—and bounced right back at them, hitting one of the officials right in the head!

The other official scissored his arms and blew his whistle. "No good!" he yelled as the first official rubbed his head and put his cap back on.

Everyone laughed—everyone except Tiki. He sank to his knees and grabbed his helmet again with both hands. His nightmare was totally coming true!

"Don't worry about it, man," Paco told him, lifting Tiki

back to his feet. "We're up 6–0. No problem! Let's go—it's time for the kickoff."

Yeah, right, Tiki thought. *The kickoff. No problem.* As he trotted down the field and placed the ball on the tee, Tiki wondered just how bad he had to be before Coach Wheeler replaced him as the kicker. Did he have to blow the whole game first?

Looking toward the sidelines, he caught Wheeler's eye. "Let's go, Tiki!" he called, clapping his hands. "You can do it!"

"No I can't," Tiki said under his breath. "That's the problem."

Still, he went ahead and lined up for the kickoff. Raising his hand high, he brought it down to signal to his teammates that he was starting his approach. He kept it simple—only four steps—to make sure he didn't whiff totally.

Just as he'd feared, he shanked the ball. Luckily it took a good bounce for the Eagles this time and ended up downed at the Mountaineers' twenty-five yard line.

My first decent kick of the day, Tiki thought—and it had been a mistake!

Tiki was actually relieved to hit the bench. Normally he couldn't wait to get out onto the field. But now the Mountaineers managed a long, slow drive, mostly consisting of running plays. By the time they scored their touchdown, the whole first quarter was gone.

The second quarter began with the score 7–6, Mountaineers. But now the Eagles pulled off a long drive of their own, featuring Tiki and John Berra on alternating plays, pounding the ball up the middle through the heart of the Mountaineers' beefy defense.

They reached the Mountaineers' fifteen yard line, but the drive faltered and the Eagles soon faced a fourth-down-and-seven situation. Tiki looked toward Coach Wheeler on the sideline, to see if he would call for the field goal attempt.

It would have been a natural call, seeing how a field goal would give the Eagles back the lead. But Wheeler signaled for them to go for the first down instead.

Tiki was relieved—but also kind of insulted! He'd just been dissed in a big way, hadn't he?

On the other hand the team needed this win. The Eagles, as they'd been reminding themselves all week, needed to win each of their remaining four games to be sure of making the play-offs. One loss—just one measly one-point loss—could mean missing out on their chance for glory.

And Tiki did not want to be the cause of that loss—no way, no how. He decided he didn't care about being dissed after all—it was better to go for it and fall short than to try a field goal and miss.

The Eagles made the first down on a short pass to Joey Gallagher, and then went on to score a touchdown on a floater to Fred Soule. The two-point conversion failed, but nobody complained that they hadn't tried the kick. Not even Tiki.

For the rest of that whole game, the only kicks he made were punts and kickoffs. When points were on the line, the Eagles did not go to their substitute kicker.

At halftime Tiki wanted to ask Coach Wheeler if he was staying away from kicking on purpose. But he didn't need to ask. Wheeler came straight over to him and admitted it.

"I can't take any chances at this point in the season," he told Tiki. "Maybe if we get a big lead . . ."

But they didn't get a big lead. The Eagles and the Mountaineers both went up and down the field the whole third quarter, yet failed to put a single point on the board.

The Mountaineers even missed on two field goal attempts. Tiki felt a pang of sympathy for the Mountaineers' kicker. *That could have been me,* he thought, relieved.

Late in the fourth quarter Ronde grabbed another interception on a third-and-long play and ran it back for his second touchdown of the game!

The two-point conversion failed—making the score Eagles 18, Mountaineers 7. This lack of extra point production turned into a near disaster for the Eagles on the next play, when the Mountaineers' returner ran back Tiki's squib kickoff for a touchdown!

And wouldn't you know it, they followed that up with a successful two-point conversion!

Now the game was back up for grabs, with the score Eagles 18, Mountaineers 15. And after three downs of going nowhere against that beefy East Side defense, the Eagles had to punt yet again.

Tiki held his breath, and practically closed his eyes as he let the kick fly. Thank goodness it somehow sailed high and true, hitting the turf behind the return man and rolling back all the way to the Mountaineers' thirty yard line!

From that moment on it was a race against the clock. The gun sounded to end the game just as the Mountaineers were racing to get their kicking squad on the field to try a game-tying field goal.

Luckily they never got it off. Tiki was sure that if they had, the poor Mountaineers' kicker would have finally put it through the uprights—something he was sure he himself could never do in a real game.

CHAPTER FIVE
MEN OF ACTION

"MAN, THAT WAS UGLY," SAID PACO AS HE TOOK OFF his shoulder pads. "I hope we never have to do that again."

"Do what?" Cody asked. "Win a game?"

"No, man," Paco replied. "Play a game without Adam."

Ronde looked over at Tiki and saw him wince. He felt bad for his twin. Ronde knew that every kid in the locker room was thinking the same thing as Paco—*including him*!

Poor Tiki, he thought. *It must really stink to be Adam's replacement.*

Tiki and Ronde rode the late bus home together. Tiki kept staring out the window at the fading evening light and the houses and stores they passed along the way.

Ronde kept staring at Tiki. He wanted to say something nice—something that would make his twin feel better. But what? What would *he* want Tiki to say to *him* if their situations were reversed?

Nothing, that's what. There was not a single thing he,

or anybody, could say that would make Tiki feel one bit better right now.

Still, he had to say something. . . . The silence was getting deafening.

"Oh, well," he finally ventured. "At least we won."

"Yeah," Tiki said, still staring out the window. "Let's just hope Adam passes his retests next week."

Ronde saw Tiki's chin tremble, and his eyes fill with tears that he blinked back fiercely. He said, "Hey, man, forget it. We won, you know? Don't worry about it."

Tiki turned to him. "Don't worry about it?" he repeated. "Are you kidding me?"

Now it was Ronde's turn to stare off into the distance. He'd tried to cheer his brother up, and he'd failed miserably—just like Tiki had as the Eagles' kicker.

"It's so unfair!" Tiki said, hitting the back of the empty seat ahead of them with his open palm. "There's *got* to be something we can do about this."

That made Ronde think. Maybe there *was* something they could do.

He kept racking his brain for an answer all the way home. He was still trying while they heated up the dinner their mom had left for them before heading off to her second job.

As they sat and ate, it finally came to Ronde. "Hey, Tiki, remember when Mom stopped that factory from getting built?"

Tiki looked up from his tuna casserole. "Yeah?"

"Well, that was unfair too, right? I mean, those builders wanted to build that factory, and they didn't care that it would pollute the neighborhood."

"So?"

"So, what I'm saying is, Mom didn't just sit there and moan about it. She rounded up a whole bunch of people to come to those meetings, and she got all those signatures on that petition, remember?"

"Yeah, so?"

"So, why don't we do the same thing, man?"

Tiki wrinkled his brow. "You mean . . . ?"

"I mean, let's get the whole team to go around school and get every kid, and every teacher, to sign a petition to let Adam back on the team!"

Tiki dropped his fork onto his plate. "You really think that'll work?"

"Hey, they didn't build that factory, did they?"

"No, they didn't . . ."

"Well? If Mom could do it, why can't we? There was only her and Mrs. Pendergast. There's fifty-something of us!"

"You really see the guys doing that?"

"Hey, dude—desperate people do desperate things, right? I mean, we can at least ask them to."

Tiki scratched his head, thinking. "You know," he said, smiling, "I hate to admit it, but every once in a while you have an idea that's worth a try!"

• • •

Convincing the team members turned out to be easy. They would have done *anything*—within reason—if it would help bring Adam back in time for the next game.

Before the end of that first lunch period, Tiki and Ronde already had the signatures of fifty-three people— all but eight of them team members.

But as they found out afterward, getting signatures from kids who weren't on the football team turned out to be a harder sell. At least that's how it was for Ronde, who had no success at all in study hall, where the teacher kept telling him to sit down and be quiet.

In his afternoon classes there was barely any time to *talk* with the other kids, let alone get them to sign something. The bell would ring, the teachers would start teaching, and then the bell would ring again and everybody would get up and scramble to their next class.

It was only after the day's final bell that Ronde had the chance to get some signatures. Unfortunately, it was raining, so most kids just made a run for the buses or cars that were waiting for them.

Ronde figured his best bet on this particular afternoon would be to go around to the various clubs, which met in classrooms after the school day was over.

There was the computer room, right across the hall. Ronde ducked inside and found a bunch of kids, some of whom he had classes with, all standing around one boy at a brand-new computer.

"Hey, Tiki," said one of the kids. "What are you doing here? Wanna join the computer club?"

Ronde thought of telling them he wasn't Tiki, but he figured it was better to let them think he was. That way, if he came off looking dumb, it would be Tiki's problem, not his.

"Um, maybe," he said.

"We'd let you in, no problem," said Jacob Tomashevski, a skinny kid with a mouthful of braces that blinded you whenever he smiled. "But, of course, you'd have to quit the football team. We meet at the same times."

"No big loss," said another computer nerd, Barbara Reese. "Sports are so dumb."

"Really," Jacob agreed. "You're too smart for that stuff, Tiki. You wanna join right now? I'll go get the application forms . . ."

"Uh, not right now, actually," Ronde said. "Thanks anyway."

"So, if you're not sure about joining the club," said a third kid whose name Ronde didn't know, "what *do* you want?"

"Um, I . . ." Now Ronde felt really stupid. They'd just made it perfectly clear what they thought of the football team. "Uh, never mind. See you guys later."

"Whatever, dude," said Jacob, shaking his head. "We'll be here. We're *always* here."

61

Ronde wiped the cold sweat from his forehead as he closed the door behind him and stepped back out into the hallway.

Okay, so he'd chickened out with those brainiacs in the computer club. But he was determined not to give up so easily next time. After all, this was his idea, wasn't it?

And besides, what would his mom have done? She surely wouldn't have quit without a fight!

He opened the door of the next classroom down the hall.

"*Oui?*" said a girl with long dark hair and big blue eyes. "*Que voulez-vous, monsieur?*"

"Uh, sorry," Ronde said. "Wrong room." He ducked back out into the hallway. He took Spanish, not French—and if these kids were gonna talk to him in a language he didn't understand, he might as well go on to the next club right now.

In another classroom he saw a bunch of kids playing chess. There were six or seven games going on at once, each with two players, and at least one or two more kids watching and commenting on the moves.

Ronde came in and said in a loud voice, "Hi, everybody!"

"Shhh!" came the reply from all two dozen chess club members.

"Can I help you?" whispered one of them, a kid with a crew cut and bad breath.

"I've . . . I've got a petition here . . . ," Ronde began.

The kid took it from him and moved off, reading it. He laughed—it was more of a snort, really—and passed it to one of the other kids who wasn't actually playing a match.

The two of them seemed to get a real kick out of Ronde's petition, all right. As it got passed along, the amusement level only went up.

"What's so funny?" Ronde asked. "It's a serious situation, believe me."

"Listen, kid," said the boy with the crew cut and the halitosis. "Nothing about the game of football could remotely be considered serious. You want a serious game, try chess." He handed Ronde's petition back to him. "I think you'd better look for signatures someplace else, my man."

"Thanks," Ronde said sarcastically, taking back his clipboard and pen. "And I'm not 'your man.' Thanks—for nothing!"

"SHHHH!" the whole room chorused as he backed out the door and slammed it behind him.

"Man," Ronde said to himself as he stuck the clipboard back into his book bag and headed for the late bus. "I hope the other kids are doing better than I am!"

As he got to the door, he stopped himself. "Wait a minute," he muttered under his breath. "I'm not gonna stand for that stuff!"

Those kids had really ticked him off. Who did they think they were? Truth was, both he and Tiki loved to play chess, and were pretty good at it. But who wanted to hang out with those bigheads?

He turned around and marched right back into the room. "You think there's nothing serious about football?" he demanded, ignoring the shushing he got from the members. "Well, let me tell you something—there's nothing more serious than sacrificing your body trying to win a ball game. Besides, we work a lot more hours on our game than you do on yours. And another thing— practicing football gets you into good shape!"

He looked at their flabby waistlines and pasty faces. "You all look like you could use a little exercise. Maybe you ought to try football sometime. If you ever gave it a chance, I bet you'd like it."

They stared at him blankly. Ronde sighed. "Look, I'm not saying chess isn't a great game. But it's no more serious than football. And if you think we don't use our brains out there on the field, you're wrong. Ask Coach Wheeler if you don't believe me. 'It's all about the mental game,' is what he always says. We do a lot of studying before we ever get out on that field."

They were still staring at him, but now they were also glancing at one another. He could feel their resistance breaking down, so he kept on going.

It was more arguing than he'd ever done in his life, but

deep in his heart he believed every word he was saying.

"Football is a *great* game," he said, "and competing against other kids helps you grow up in a lot of ways. You all ought to know that—I mean, chess is a competitive game too.

"Well, our chances to get into the play-offs rest completely on our kicker being there for us. And the school won't let him play, just because he flunked a couple tests in math and science."

"Whoa, now hold up there," said the kid with the crew cut. "Schoolwork is more important than meaningless things like sports."

"Are you counting chess as a sport?" Ronde shot back.

That caught the other kid by surprise. "I, um . . ."

"Okay, school's more important—that's true," said Ronde, "but suspending Adam from the Eagles is punishing the whole team for one kid's mistake. Is that fair?"

Silence.

"I promise you guys, if you sign this and Adam gets to play the rest of the season, I'll personally guarantee that he'll pass all his tests. Is that good enough for you?"

They all looked at one another. "Sounds good to me," said crew cut. "How 'bout you guys?"

"I'm in," said one of the players.

"Me too," said another, whom Ronde recognized from

English class. "Hey, Tiki. You know, if football doesn't work out for you, you've got a real future on the debating team!"

"*How* many?" Tiki asked, amazed.

"Seventy-three signatures," Ronde said proudly. "How about you?"

"Um, I only got forty-seven," Tiki admitted.

"Hey, that's not bad!" Ronde said, pleased. "If everybody else did as good as we did, Adam's gonna be back on the team for sure!"

The team members all gathered at the cafeteria table at lunchtime on Tuesday to count up their signatures. Among the fifteen of them who'd volunteered to get names, they'd collected 393!

"That's out of nine hundred kids in the whole school!" Cody said excitedly.

"You think we should keep at it till tomorrow?" Paco asked.

"No, man," Ronde said, taking charge. "We don't have time to mess around. Besides, it's just as good if we go into Dr. Anand's office and show her how many names we got in just two days. She'll be able to do the math from there."

"Dude, she'll *have* to let Adam back on the team now!" Fred said, pumping his fist and slapping Cody five.

• • •

They were all sure that the principal would be impressed with the haul of signatures they'd brought in. And she was.

"I want to commend you boys for your caring, and for your spirit of activism. I'm going to see to it that you all get Good Citizenship certificates as a reward."

"That's great, Dr. Anand," Ronde said, giving Tiki a sideways glance. "Thank you."

It was just the two of them in there with the principal. The team had decided it was better that way, rather than all of them crowding in and shouting at once.

"But I'm afraid the rule still stands. I cannot allow Adam to return to game action until he's passed both his failed tests. It would send the wrong signal about the importance of academics at this school, and I cannot have that."

"*Please*, Dr. Anand?" Tiki begged. "We really need him."

"You don't realize what this will do to the team!" Ronde pleaded. "It's going to crush our morale!"

She sighed sadly. "I know you all find this upsetting, and I don't blame you one bit. I'm sure too that if the Eagles don't make the play-offs, I'll be blamed by many of the children, not to mention parents and coaches. But I feel I have no choice. It's not just that rules are rules; it's that this particular rule is there for a very good reason."

Ronde bit down hard on his lip to keep from saying

something he'd regret later. But Tiki just couldn't help himself.

"Man—this is so wrong!" he moaned.

"I'm sorry, Ronde," said Dr. Anand, mistaking him for his brother, as people so often did. "I hope someday you'll understand."

Tiki marched out, not bothering to answer her. "He's just upset," Ronde explained.

"I know," said Dr. Anand. "I'm sure you are too. Thank you, Tiki."

"Um . . ." He was about to correct her, but he figured he'd let Tiki take the credit this time.

"If you boys *really* want Adam back on the team," she said as he was opening the door to go, "I suggest you encourage him to study hard. I'm sure he could use the moral support, even though he's being tutored."

"Yes, ma'am," Ronde said, and closed the door behind him.

"Well," he told Tiki, putting an arm on his shoulder as they walked back to the locker room, where the team was waiting, "at least we tried."

Tiki looked back at him hopelessly. "Okay, genius," he said. "Now what do we do?"

Ronde picked a clump of turf out of his face mask and tossed it to the ground. "Yo, Fred," he said to the Eagles' wideout, who'd just landed on top of him. "Get off me, man."

"Sorry, Ronde," Fred said, helping him up. "I was just going for the ball."

"Me too, yo!" Ronde shot back. "It's only a scrimmage, remember? You don't have to kill me."

Fred laughed, and so did Ronde. They were good friends by now, even though Fred was a ninth grader, and even though he was on offense and Ronde on defense.

The Eagles had become a close-knit family, especially after all they'd been through at the start of the season, when Coach Spangler had suddenly deserted them to coach the high school team.

There was still a lot of tension under all that team closeness, though. They all knew what their lousy start meant. It was November now, and they were still in the play-off hunt, but barely.

Only *one more loss* and their destiny would be out of their hands. So it was no surprise that they played hard in practice—almost as hard as in real games.

Today's scrimmage had an extra edge to it. They all knew Adam was inside the school building at that very moment, taking his makeup tests after a week of tutoring and mental torture.

Tiki was at the far end of the field with Coach Wheeler. Tiki's kicks were looking much better, Ronde thought. Mr. Wheeler seemed upbeat about it, too, clapping his hands and shouting encouragement.

The rest of the team was scrimmaging—the offense

against the defense. But without Tiki the offense was at only half its normal strength.

Ronde worried that Tiki wasn't getting his regular repetitions on offense. He might do great at kicking this week against the Blue Ridge Bears—but that Bears' offense, one of the best around, was going to score points off them.

The Eagles, Ronde knew, would have to answer with points of their own. And that meant touchdowns, not just field goals.

If Tiki was off his running game, there was no way John Berra could take up the slack. And without their ground game going, the Eagles could easily lose this contest to a much better squad than they'd faced the week before.

Ronde and the others were lining up for another play when the locker room doors swung open and Mrs. Franklin appeared, grim-faced. Everyone stopped still and stared her way. Holding Adam's test papers in her hand, she slowly shook her head from side to side.

Later, looking at a video with the rest of the defense, Ronde watched the Blue Ridge Bears' previous game. He paid particular attention to their big wide receiver, Chris Jones.

"He's been All-State the past two seasons," Coach Wheeler told them. "Their quarterback loves to throw it up for grabs for him, because of that height advantage and those good, soft hands."

"Don't worry, Coach," Ronde said grimly. "He's not scoring off me. That is just not going to happen."

"Well, I know you can get up there with the best of them, Ronde," Coach Wheeler replied. "But it'll help if you give him a good bump at the line of scrimmage, to throw him off his routes."

"Got it," Ronde said intently.

"You'll have to be alert," the coach added. "Because Giordano's a scrambler. If he rolls out your way, you'll have to make a quick decision which way to go. It's a challenge, Ronde. You up to it?"

"You know I am, Coach."

But he wasn't so sure about Tiki.

CHAPTER SIX

GAME-CHANGER

"YESSSS!" TIKI COULDN'T HELP SHOUTING FOR JOY as he watched his opening kickoff sail high and long, just like one of Adam's. Finally—FINALLY—he'd made a really good kick that wasn't just for practice.

The return man grabbed the kick, but before he could make a move, Ronde came crashing into him, sending him backward a full five yards before he toppled to the ground.

"Barber City!" Tiki yelled, clapping his hands as he headed for the sidelines.

He sat and watched as the Bears tried two weak runs into the Eagles' line. Sam Scarfone dropped the runner for a loss on first down, and the second run netted only three yards. "Here comes a pass," Cody told Tiki as they sat side by side.

Tiki shaded his eyes from the setting sun of that late Thursday afternoon. He tried to make out Ronde as he lined up opposite the Bears' best receiver.

"Are you kidding me?" Tiki gasped. "That kid's got to be six feet tall! What are they feeding them over there?"

"I hear their cafeteria sells martian food," Cody cracked. But before Tiki could think of a comeback, the play started, and both boys watched Ronde make a desperate leap, batting the long pass away at the last second.

"Whew!" Cody said, shaking his head. "That would have been six points for sure."

It was true, Tiki knew. He also knew that the Bears would keep coming back to that play all day long. Their receiver, Chris Jones, had at least seven inches on Ronde, and the Bears would surely try to cash in.

Now, though, it was time for the Eagles to take over. Tiki strapped on his helmet and took to the field with the rest of the offense.

Coach Wheeler had planned to feature the running game today, because he wanted to use up as much clock as possible, to keep the dangerous Bears offense off the field.

But the Bears must have known what the Eagles were up to, because every time Cody gave Tiki the ball, the defense was on him in a flash. Even when Tiki went out for a pass, there were two men on him at all times.

It was the first time all year that a team had chosen to double-team Tiki. It made him feel proud in a way—honored. But he wished they'd stop it, because it was mad hard to get anything done with two men on him instead of one!

Maybe if the Eagles' offense had been crisper—if their timing had been perfect—they could have overcome the problem. But Tiki hadn't practiced with the rest of the group all week. He and Cody seemed to be on different pages all the time, or maybe even reading from different books.

The handoffs were late in coming, so that by the time Tiki secured the ball, the hole in the line had already closed. Or else they were early and Tiki wound up bobbling the ball and barely holding on before being blasted behind the line of scrimmage.

In the bad old days Cody would have been all over him about it. But things were different now. The Eagles were a team, and they supported one another, no matter what.

Although they didn't score during the whole first half, the Eagles did manage to keep hold of the ball for a big chunk of time.

Tiki's punts were long and high, too—Paco and the rest of the line did a great job of holding off the pressure. So the Bears were always operating deep in their own territory. And good old Ronde was doing his part, keeping the Bears' big receiver from making any long gains.

With less than a minute left in the half, Tiki was feeling pretty good about things. They'd weathered the Bears' attack. They just had to figure out a way to score in the second half. And Tiki was sure Coach Wheeler would have some ideas.

But with only twenty seconds left, disaster struck. Sam

Scarfone came on a third down blitz, but let the Bears' quarterback slip out of his grasp and scramble free.

Meanwhile, Ronde had kept close to his man for as long as he could. But once the Bears' quarterback started scrambling, Ronde had to make a choice—and he chose to stop the pass. And that allowed the quarterback to tuck the ball under his arm and run for the end zone.

As soon as he saw Giordano pass the line of scrimmage, Tiki knew the Eagles were in trouble. They were all bunched up at the line, with both wide receivers way downfield.

Nobody on the Eagles' defense was fast enough to catch the quarterback now—nobody except Ronde. But Ronde got blindsided by the big receiver he'd been covering, and knocked flat on his face while Giordano raced down the sideline all the way to the end zone!

"NOOOOOO!" Tiki shouted. But it didn't do any good. The kick for the extra point went right down the middle. Halftime came too late, and the score was Bears 7, Eagles 0.

In the visitors' locker room, Tiki sat on the bench, dejected. He wasn't the only one. "Man!" he said. "How many yards did I rush for? Only thirty-five? That is pathetic!"

"Hey, Tiki," Cody said, putting an arm around his shoulder. "We all stunk that half. But we've got time to turn it around."

This was the new Cody—a real leader, not a conceited phony. And Coach Wheeler backed him right up. "Okay, gang," he said. "That was just a fluke play right there."

"I should have sacked him," Sam said, shaking his head miserably.

"You almost did," Paco said, patting Sam on the shoulder. "You'll get him next time. Don't worry."

"That's right," Coach Wheeler agreed. "Just remember, he's a tricky one. You never know where he's going to come from. Now, here are some things we can do to turn this game around in the second half . . ."

"Go, Ronde! GOOOO!"

Tiki shouted his lungs out, jumping up and down with the rest of them as Ronde took the opening kickoff and ran it back all the way to the Bears' twenty-five yard line!

Now it was up to the offense. Tiki couldn't wait to get the ball back in his hands and run it right down the Bears' throats!

But Coach Wheeler had seen enough in the first half to make him change the offensive game plan. For this drive Cody was told to throw the ball on every down.

Tiki did catch one pass—for a gain of six on first down—but that was the only time he touched the ball, as the Eagles drove through the air for their first touchdown of the day.

True, it was Tiki's key block on the Bears' blitzing linebacker that allowed Cody to find Fred Soule in the end zone on third down. If not for that block, it would have been sack city, and Tiki would probably have had to try for a field goal. Not a pretty picture.

Fred spiked the ball, and the rest of the Eagles whooped it up. They were right back in the game!

Tiki was in midcelebration along with the rest of them when he realized Coach Wheeler was calling for him to kick an extra point.

Somehow the call caught him completely off guard. In the last game, after his first muffed attempt, Coach had called for two-point conversions every single time. Obviously, seeing how well Tiki had kicked the ball in the first half of this game had changed Coach's mind.

Tiki felt a sudden cold sweat break out on his forehead. Goose bumps stood up on his arms and the back of his neck. This extra point would either tie the game or leave the Eagles trailing. It might even be the point that made the difference between making or not making the play-offs!

For weeks the Eagles had been living on the razor's edge, in constant must-win situations. And now it was getting even more tense!

Tiki felt like he was going to faint. "You okay?" Joey Gallagher asked him.

"Fine. I'm fine," Tiki managed to say as he lined up to make the kick.

Here came the snap. There came the rushers. And here went Tiki, launching the kick straight at the uprights—but *too low*!

BANG! The ball hit the crossbar, just like it had the week before. But this time, amazingly, it bounced up and through!

He'd done it! Tiki sank to his knees, feeling wobbly and weak. His teammates hoisted him back to his feet and smacked him on the back and on the helmet.

"Good job, dude!" they shouted. "Hey, you sure you're not Costa's long-lost brother?"

"Hey, Tiki," Ronde said, coming up to him and looking him straight in the eye through their face masks. "You okay, man? You look weird."

"I *feel* weird," Tiki admitted.

"Well, get it together, bro. You've got to kick off now."

"Oh. Yeah. Right."

Tiki breathed deeply, and tried to shake the cobwebs out of his giddy head. "Okay. Here goes nothing."

The kickoff somehow went fine. It was low and end-over-end, but it did the job, nailing the Bears deep in their own territory.

The Eagles' defense had no problem keeping them bottled up in their own zone, and soon it was the Eagles' ball again, this time at midfield.

Coach Wheeler signaled for yet another pass play on first down. Tiki was disappointed. If only Coach would give him a chance, he was sure he could outwit the double-team.

Cody's pass fell incomplete, and so did the next two. Once again the Eagles' offense had gone nowhere. Tiki sure hoped that on the next drive, Coach Wheeler would go back to the running game.

But right then it was time to punt. Once again Tiki had to shift roles and change his focus. He was beginning to realize just how hard it was to play two positions in one game.

All day long Tiki's kicks had been smooth and easy. Until that last extra point had hit the crossbar, he hadn't even felt the jitters he'd experienced the week before. But now the Bears sent every man they had at Tiki, to try to block the punt.

Tiki had had no clue they would be coming—and when he saw them rushing at him, he panicked. If he'd just ignored them and made the kick, he would have gotten it off easily. But by the time he came out of his frozen stupor, they were almost on him!

At the last second he let his instincts take over. Instead of trying to kick into the wall of onrushing Bears, he tucked the ball under his arm and morphed back into a running back!

He juked and jived, deked and spun, and somehow, blindly, jitterbugged his way into the open field!

The Bears all skidded to a halt and turned to chase

Tiki, but by now it was too late. They'd sent everyone in to block the kick except the return man, and he was the only player left with a chance to stop Tiki.

Make that *no* chance.

Even though he didn't really need to, Tiki dove head-long into the end zone, his arms holding the ball stretched way out in front of him.

His goof had turned into gold! TOUCHDOWN!

"YAAAAAA!" he screamed as he danced around with the ball held high over his head. Then he spiked it and jumped into his teammates' arms. They trotted off the field together, laughing and shouting.

"Attaboy, Tiki!" Coach Wheeler said, smacking him on the back. "We're gonna put that play in on purpose next week!"

"There'd better not be another week of this!" Tiki shot back, laughing and breathing hard. He felt dizzy, so he lay down on the bench to get his wind back.

"No, no, no. Get back up, dude!" Ronde yelled at him. "Time for the extra point!"

"Huh? Oh, right!" Tiki got back up, steadied himself, and went over to Coach Wheeler's side. "Hey, Coach, how 'bout a two-point conversion this time?"

Coach shook his head. "No, Tiki. No more messing around. You can do it, kid. You just did it five minutes ago, remember?"

"Barely."

"Never mind. Just get out there and stick it, okay?"

"Okay."

Coach must have heard the hesitation in Tiki's voice, because he grabbed both sides of his helmet and looked him right in the eye. "Just stay cool, okay? Concentrate."

Tiki nodded, and ran back out onto the field. But he was still breathing hard. The goalposts seemed to be swaying, and he could feel himself go off balance as he launched into the kick.

The whistle blew before Tiki knew what had happened. But the groans from his teammates told him all he needed to know.

The extra point was no good!

Even worse, now he had to go and kick off again. Tiki's heart was in his throat, and his heartbeat was thundering loudly in his ears. Every breath made a whooshing sound like a hurricane. He swallowed, trying to "pop" his ears, but it only worked for a second or two each time. He tried to take deep breaths, but they only made him see stars.

"Okay, steady, steady," he muttered under his breath. "And . . . go!" He held his right arm up, then brought it down, signaling the start of his kick to his teammates.

He ran at the ball, swung his foot forward, and booted it low and long. Tiki stood watching as it landed right in the arms of the return man.

Oh, no! Tiki thought. The ball had gotten there so quickly that a line of Bears' blockers had time to form in front of the returner. Tiki had trouble seeing where the returner was—until he suddenly spurted free along the far sideline!

Tiki gasped—he was the only Eagle left who could prevent a touchdown!

He raced after the kid, trying to cut the diagonal and tackle him before he reached the goal line. But it was too late, and there was just too much ground to cover.

Touchdown, Blue Ridge Bears!

The extra point was no problem for their kicker. And now the Eagles trailed again, 14–13, in a game where losing was not an option.

And yet, as drive after drive was stalled by the stubborn defenses of both teams, and the clock wound down to two minutes left, losing began to seem like a definite possibility.

The Eagles had the ball on their own thirty-four, with only one time-out left. Cody brought the troops together in the huddle. "Okay, now. Ohio State on three."

The screen pass.

Tiki faked a block, then drifted to the weak side and saw the ball come toward him. He grabbed it and swung left to avoid a bruising hit by the linebacker. Darting forward, he made it into the secondary, and wound up carrying two defensive backs all the way to the fifty yard line!

Back in the huddle Cody said, "Texas Tech on four."

A running play up the middle. *Could Coach Wheeler really have called that play?* Tiki wondered. It would eat up a lot of clock, after all—and they needed to *stop* the clock, not keep it going!

"No, man, we've got to pass!" Tiki said urgently.

"Coach must have seen something they're doing," Paco assured him.

"Hey, it's Coach's call," Cody said, and that was that.

Sure enough, there was a hole in the Bears' line that hadn't been there before—a hole big enough for Tiki to squirt through and dart all the way to the Bears' thirty-five!

But now there were only forty seconds left, and the clock was running. After two incomplete passes in the end zone, the Eagles found themselves with only twenty seconds in which to save their season from going off a cliff.

It was third and ten, and Coach Wheeler sent John Berra in with the play. "Penn State, on two."

Penn State was a short, quick pass to Tiki in the right flat. As they lined up and he got into his stance, Tiki realized that Coach Wheeler was putting the game in his hands. He could almost hear him saying, *Tiki, I'm giving you the ball here. Either score us a touchdown or it'll be up to you to kick the winning field goal. So . . . which is it gonna be?*

Tiki gulped. He *had* to score a touchdown; he just

had to! Desperate, he grabbed the pass and headed for pay-dirt with every ounce of energy and spirit he could muster.

It got him only to the seven yard line.

"Time-out!" Cody screamed, and the refs blew the whistle with only three seconds left.

"Field goal!" Coach Wheeler called out.

Tiki did the math—it would be a twenty-four yard attempt. Not hugely long, if you were Adam Costa—but not a gimme either.

"Go, Tiki!" he heard Ronde shouting as he lined up to make the kick.

The ball was snapped. Tiki launched the kick. It was up . . . and it was . . .

No good!

His kick had been long enough but not high enough. It fell just underneath the crossbar, only a foot or two short.

No good. No good. NO GOOD!

Tiki took off his helmet, sank to his knees, and buried his head in his hands. The Eagles had lost again—and it was all his fault!

Now their destiny was completely out of their hands. Unless some kind of miracle happened, they'd *never* make it to the play-offs!

CHAPTER SEVEN

DESPERATE MEASURES

RONDE WATCHED THE KICK FALL SHORT, AND suddenly he felt like a huge rock had been dropped right on top of him. He stood there stunned, helmet in hand, tears streaming down his face.

His teammates stood like a group of statues, staring into the distance, frozen in disbelief.

Now that the game was over, Ronde realized he'd known, deep in his heart, that from the moment they'd lost Adam the Eagles had been clinging to life by the thinnest of threads.

Now that thread had broken, and they were falling, falling off the cliff, with the play-offs slipping far out of reach.

"It's over," Sam said dully as they trudged back into the locker room and collapsed onto the wooden benches. "There goes our season."

"Don't let me hear you say that!" Coach Wheeler said sharply. "Don't ever let me hear any of you talk like that. We've still got a chance to make the play-offs—that's what the math says, and that's what I say too.

"As long as we're mathematically alive, I don't want to hear any more about us not making it. And if I catch any of you guys sulking, or playing half-baked football like you don't care anymore, you can do your sulking from the bench! Is that clear?"

For a moment nobody answered. Finally Cody said, "Yes, Coach," and the rest of them all muttered "Yes, Coach" too.

Ronde felt lower than he could ever remember feeling—so he could only imagine how his twin was feeling right then.

Say, where *was* he, anyway? "Anybody seen Tiki?" Nobody had, and nobody seemed like they wanted to get up and look for him either.

Ronde went back out onto the field, and right away he saw his brother. Tiki was sitting on his helmet, right by the uprights at the back of the end zone. His chin was propped up in both hands, and he was staring straight out at the field.

"Hey," Ronde said, sitting down next to him.

"Hey," Tiki said in a hoarse whisper.

"You okay?"

"No. Are you?"

"Not really."

"This is the worst thing that's ever happened."

"Come on, Tiki. You know that's not true."

"Oh, no?"

"I mean, nobody got hurt or anything."

"Not on the *outside*."

"Tiki, man, you did the best you could. It's not like you told anybody you wanted to be the kicker."

"I should have nailed it, Ronde," Tiki said. "It was an easy kick."

Ronde didn't answer. There was nothing more to say about it. Instead he asked, "You coming inside?"

Tiki sighed. "I feel like walking home."

"Are you serious? We're all the way on the other side of town."

"It's a good thing too," Tiki said. "Can you imagine if this was a home game? At least I didn't choke in front of every single person I know."

"Come on, dude, let's go. The bus is gonna leave soon."

Tiki hesitated. "Are they all mad at me?"

"Who, the team? No, man—they understand."

"They do?"

"Totally. It's not your fault."

"It's not?"

"No, Tiki. Don't think like that."

"How should I think, then?" Tiki shook his head. "You know," he said, "I'll bet Adam feels even worse than I do."

"You got that right," Ronde agreed. "And wait till he hears about us losing this game."

"Man, he's *got* to get back on this team," Tiki said. "He's just *got* to!"

"What is the *matter* with you two?" Mrs. Barber asked. "You've been down all weekend."

"It's the team, Mom," Tiki said. "I cost us the game on Thursday, and now we're just about out of the play-offs."

"First of all, Tiki," she said, "one player doesn't lose the game; the whole team does. It's a team sport, remember?"

"She's right, bro," Ronde agreed. But he noticed it didn't make Tiki feel any better.

"And second of all," Mrs. Barber went on, "'just about' out of the play-offs? What do you mean, 'just about'?"

"He means unless the Bears and the Colts lose both their last two games, we can't catch up," Ronde explained.

"And they're not *going* to lose twice," Tiki added. "They've got totally easy schedules the rest of the way."

"Well, maybe they'll surprise you," Mrs. Barber said gently. "One team may be favored over another, but you never know. Like the coach says, 'That's why they play the games.'"

She smiled, and gave each of them a kiss on the forehead. "It's way too early for you boys to start feeling down. Why, you're defeating yourselves before you've even played the games!"

Ronde shot Tiki a look. They both knew their mom was right—*as usual*.

As she was about to leave the room, she turned and said, "You know who *really* has good reason to be down, don't you? Your friend Adam, that's who."

Ronde felt as though someone had suddenly shaken him awake.

"Adam?" Tiki repeated.

"Yes, Adam—your old friend. Remember him? What does *he* have to say about all this? Has anybody asked him lately how he's doing?"

Ronde looked at the floor. Then he snuck a glance at Tiki, who was looking right back at him guiltily.

Tiki shrugged. "We haven't really seen him much."

"He's been kind of busy," Ronde added. "You know, studying and stuff."

"Has he been avoiding you?" their mom asked.

"Well, he doesn't come to the cafeteria anymore at lunchtime," Tiki said.

"I guess that's when he gets tutored," Ronde said. "And when you see him in the hall, he doesn't say much—just 'hi,' and stuff like that, you know?"

"*Adam Costa*?" Mrs. Barber said, astonished. "Why, of all your friends he's got to be the biggest talker!"

"Not anymore," Ronde said. "Not since he flunked those tests."

"And he's not at the practices or the games," Tiki

added. "So we don't get to see that much of him."

"Maybe he doesn't show up to watch because he's afraid you're all *mad* at him," Mrs. Barber said. "Did you ever think of that?"

He hadn't, Ronde had to admit. Truth was, for the past two weeks he'd been trying hard not to think about Adam. Now he felt ashamed of himself for neglecting his friend.

After their mom left the room, Tiki turned to Ronde and said, "Now I feel bad."

"Me too," Ronde agreed.

"I know Adam must be feeling low."

"Lower than dirt," Ronde said, nodding.

"But what are we supposed to do about it?" Tiki asked.

Ronde thought hard. "I guess we could call him up. You know, ask him how he's doing."

"Offer a little moral support," Tiki added.

"Right. And maybe . . ." Ronde fell silent, remembering something his mom had said back when this whole mess had started.

"What?" Tiki prodded him.

"I was just thinking . . ."

"Of?"

"You know how we offered to help Adam study?"

"Yeah, but he told us he was already getting tutored, remember?"

"Doesn't seem to be doing him any good, does it?" Ronde asked pointedly, staring at the telephone.

There was a moment when both boys sat as silent and still as statues. Then, as if they were pouncing on a fumbled football, they both jumped for the phone. Tiki grabbed it away just as Ronde was about to grab it.

"Okay, okay. *I'll* pick up in the living room this time," Ronde said, admitting defeat. He stuck his tongue out at Tiki, who laughed as he dialed Adam's number.

Ronde picked up the extension just as Tiki was asking Mrs. Costa if Adam could come to the phone.

"He's studying, Tiki," she said. "I don't want to disturb him."

"But this is important!" Tiki said. "Just for a minute? Please?"

"I'm sorry," she said, holding her ground. "You can talk to him in school tomorrow." She hung up before either of the boys could say anything else.

Ronde went back into the kitchen. "Wait till tomorrow? I don't think so. This is too important."

"Let's ride over there on our bikes," Tiki suggested. Ten minutes later they were staring up at Adam's bedroom window. Tiki grabbed a tiny pebble and tossed it.

"Hey!" Ronde said. "You're gonna break that window!"

"Did I break it?" Tiki asked.

"Not that time, but—"

"Then don't bug me, all right?"

Luckily, the window opened before Tiki got another chance to prove Ronde right. Adam popped his head out, squinted behind his thick glasses at the bright sunshine, and called, "Who's there?"

"It's us!" Ronde shouted. "Hey, man, why does your mom have you locked up there like that?"

"She says I don't get to have any fun till I pass those retests."

"That is cold, dude," Tiki said, shaking his head. "How can a person think without having some fun once in a while?"

"That's what *I* said!" Adam agreed. "And you know what *she* said? She said, 'I don't want your mind clear—I want it stuffed full of knowledge!'"

"Is it working?" Ronde asked.

"Well, it's stuffed, all right," Adam said. "So stuffed, it feels like it's spinning."

"How are you doing otherwise?" Tiki asked.

Adam cocked his head sideways. "What do you mean?"

"You know what he means," Ronde said. "Are you okay?"

"You mean, *okay* okay?"

"Yeah."

"No. Of course I'm not okay! I'm such a loser that I made losers out of my whole team!"

"Don't talk like that, man," Ronde said. "We know you're trying hard to get back."

"Come on," Adam said. "You know everybody's mad at me. Even you guys. You don't have to lie."

"Everyone's mad at the *principal*, not *you!*" Tiki said.

"Yeah, right," Adam said, unconvinced.

"So . . ." Ronde said. "Do you think you're gonna make it back for next game?"

"I . . . I don't know . . ."

"Man, if we lose one more—," Tiki began.

"I can't help it! My tutor's a total jerk. She makes me feel like some freak."

"You're not a freak," Ronde said. "Except for your kicking foot, that is."

"I just can't get this stuff through my thick skull," Adam said. "And the more I try, the less I seem to get it."

Ronde and Tiki exchanged a worried glance. Then Ronde said, "Hey, Adam, why don't Tiki and I try tutoring you instead? He's good in Biology, and I'm a math whiz, as you already know. I'll bet we could help you."

Adam picked his head up and looked down at them. "You . . . You guys mean it?"

"Hey," Tiki replied, "we offered before, and you said no."

"Yeah," Adam said. "I figured, you know, she's a ninth grader, I'll be better off with her. Obviously not, right? I mean, I failed my makeup tests. You know what I think the problem is? She took all this stuff a year ago. She's forgotten more of it than I know!"

They all laughed. It was good to see Adam acting like his old self, cracking jokes and making everyone laugh.

Now, thought Ronde, if only he and Tiki could get him those passing grades.

It was Ronde's turn first. They met in an empty classroom during lunch period. Adam had volunteered to bring sandwiches from home so they wouldn't have to waste any time on the food line.

"Okay, now. Show me where you're stuck," Ronde began.

"Well, it's not just one thing. It's pretty much everything. But I think if I could get down with making up equations, I could do the other stuff. Problem is, it takes me so long to do them that I run out of time on the test before I'm finished, and that's why I can't pass."

"But, dude," Ronde said, "making up equations is easy!"

"Easy for you, maybe."

"No, man. Come on, let's do one together. You'll see how easy it is."

Adam shrugged and sighed. "Okay, have it your way. Here's one that's been turning my brains into yogurt for the last hour." He shoved a textbook toward Ronde and pointed out the problem in question.

"Okay. Fine." Ronde read the problem out loud.

"Model an equation for cost (c) given x pounds of fruit salad at \$3.50 per pound and y cans of tuna at \$1.29 per can. Hmmm . . ."

"See what I mean?" Adam asked, raising an eyebrow.

Rondo was already scribbling notes, figuring out how to write the equation. "There you go," he said, turning the paper so Adam could see it. "C = 3.50x + 1.29y."

"Huh? How'd you come up with that?"

Ronde tried to explain, but he could see that it was only making Adam more confused than before.

"I just can't concentrate!" Adam moaned, slamming down his pencil and sighing deeply. He rubbed his eyes with the palms of his hands and yanked at his hair. "Doh! It's too hard! I'm breaking out in a cold sweat here, Ronde! Let's face it. My tutor was right. I'm never going to get this stuff through my head."

"Hey—never mind what she said. *I'm* your tutor now, and I'm telling you, you're *not* stupid. Just concentrate, okay?"

"I'm trying—it's just not working!'"

"Now, don't give up!" Ronde pleaded. "That's not like you, Adam! Hey, when the Eagles are down three points with a minute left to go, do we give up?"

Adam snorted. "No way!"

"Right—and why don't we give up?"

"Because all we have to do is kick a field goal."

"Exactly."

"What's that got to do with anything?"

"Stay with me now," Ronde urged him. "Let's forget about tuna fish and fruit salad."

"Good. They don't go together anyway."

"And let's pretend it's an equation about football, okay?"

"Okay . . . I guess."

Ronde thought hard for a moment, then said, "Suppose we had to come up with an equation describing the total number of points our team scored this season, based on the number of touchdowns and field goals."

"What about extra points?" Adam asked.

"You're automatic on those, dude, so we'll just figure each touchdown as seven points, okay?"

"Cool. Now what?"

"Well, could you write down an equation that expressed that? You can use any letters you want for touchdowns and field goals. That's why they call them variables."

"Um, okay. . . . Let's see . . ." Adam squinted his eyes and started tapping on the table with his pencil. Then he wrote: $P = 7t + 3f$. "Is that right?" he asked, adding, "t is for the number of touchdowns and f is—"

"I get it, I get it," Ronde said, examining Adam's handiwork. "Yeah, man, that's right! You did it!"

"You're kidding."

"No, I'm not kidding. You did it perfectly!"

"I did?"

"See, you really do know how to do this stuff. You're just having problems concentrating on anything but football!"

Adam blew out a big breath. "You got that right," he agreed.

"Now, what about safeties?" Ronde said.

"Safeties?"

"Two points each. I know we've scored one or two of those this year. How would you add that to the equation?"

"Let's see . . ." Adam did some more scribbling. "Like this?"

"$P = 7t + 3f + 2s$. Perfect! Dude, you're gonna ace that makeup test!"

They high-fived each other.

"Wow!" Adam said. "I actually did it!"

"See, you don't need a new brain," Ronde told him. "You just have to use the brain you've already got!"

"Hey, Ronde," Adam said, smiling, "you know, if you don't end up in the NFL, you would make an awesome teacher someday!"

"Yeah, right," Ronde said. "Now that we've got that straight, let's move on to the tuna fish and fruit salad."

CHAPTER EIGHT
THE RAZOR'S EDGE

TIKI LAUNCHED A PERFECT KICK AT THE UPRIGHTS from the twenty yard line. "And it's good!" he shouted, clapping his hands and smiling.

Joey Gallagher got up from his crouch, and Paco came over to share high fives.

"That's three in a row, dude," said Paco. "Now all you've gotta do is do it in an actual game."

"No problem," Joey said. "Tiki's in the groove now."

Tiki accepted their congratulations, but inside he didn't feel much better. He knew what they all knew but nobody dared to say—that when the game was on the line, none of what he did in practice mattered one little bit.

Every time he'd gotten the chance to kick some points onto the scoreboard in an actual game, he'd gone and blown it!

Well, maybe not every *single* time—but he'd been bad enough that the team had lost its crucial third game—the one big loss that might well send them home instead of to the play-offs.

Worse, if Tiki couldn't get it together this next game, the Eagles might lose that one too! That would be the absolute final blow to Hidden Valley's season.

"How's it going, Tiki?" Coach Wheeler asked as the three boys came over to the sideline.

"Good, I guess," Tiki said, looking away.

"Where's Ronde today? Out sick?"

"Nah," Tiki said. "He's tutoring Adam for his math makeup test. It's my turn next week, in biology."

"Oh! Good!" said the coach. "Let's hope he nails them."

The other boys went to their lockers, and Coach Wheeler walked along with Tiki over to the watercooler. Here, they were far from the rest of the team and coaches, and no one could hear what they said.

"Hey, listen, Tiki," the coach said. "I really do admire you and your brother. It's not every kid who'll take time away from football to do something big for a friend."

"We're doing it for the team, too," Tiki pointed out. "Maybe *mostly* for the team."

Coach Wheeler smiled and shook his head. "Doesn't matter—it's still a good deed, and especially for Adam. You should both feel very proud."

Tiki shrugged and looked at the ground. "I guess."

"What's wrong?" the coach asked. "What's bothering you, kid?"

Tiki looked up into the coach's eagle eyes. "No matter

what happens, Adam won't be back in time for this next game."

"Ah. I see. You're afraid you're going to mess up our kicking game, and that we'll get eliminated because of it. Right?"

"Yeah," Tiki admitted. "That's pretty much it. I mean, I've already just about killed our chances."

"That's ridiculous," Wheeler said.

"You think so? I don't."

"Well, look, Tiki," said the coach, "we are where we are. Yesterday is ancient history. You're our kicker this next game, and we have to make the best of that. Let's just hope we win this one and get Adam back for the last one."

"Yeah, but the last one won't even matter if we lose this one!"

"It'll still matter to *Adam*," Coach Wheeler pointed out. "Now let's talk about the game, okay?"

"Coach," Tiki pleaded, "please don't make me kick anymore!"

"Listen to me, Tiki. You can do this! I've *seen* you do it! Remember, the team needs you!"

"But I stink at kicking! I lost us the last game on an easy field goal I should have made. And I miss half my extra points, too."

Coach Wheeler frowned, deep in thought. "Look," he said, "*somebody* has to do the punts and kickoffs. Just do the best you can. As for the field goals . . . Well, let's hope we don't have to try for any. And all right—we'll go for two on every touchdown."

"Great!" said Tiki, and took a deep breath of relief. "And can I fake some punts?"

Wheeler frowned again. "I don't think so, Tiki. We can't afford to be backed up into our own zone."

"We *won't* be, Coach! I have a much better chance of running it for a first down than I do of making a decent punt."

One corner of the coach's mouth turned up in a crooked grin, and his eagle eyes twinkled. "All right. I'll flash you the high sign. That'll be the signal you're free to pull a fake."

He stuck out his hand, and Tiki shook it so hard Wheeler had to laugh. "So, are we good to go now?"

"Good to go?" Tiki said. "I'm totally psyched!"

Tiki was glad they were all the way across town for this game against the Badgers of William Byrd Junior High. The pressure was always a lot higher when your mom and your friends and everyone you knew was sitting there watching.

Today would be tough enough without that added pressure. Just knowing that if they lost they were mathematically eliminated was enough to make every member of the team—especially Tiki—as jumpy as a high voltage cable.

This might be our last meaningful game this season, Tiki thought. And if they lost, it would be William Byrd, of all teams, that had ruined their season—starting with that horrible one-point loss at home in their very first game, when they'd had no real coach and it had been every man for himself.

The Badgers had a losing record—2–8—but one of those two victories had been that early shocker against the Eagles. *If they beat us again*, thought Tiki, *it'll be really tough to take.*

Well, at least he could forget about trying to score points with his foot. It was a relief that Coach Wheeler had agreed to stay away from field goals and extra-point kicks. On punts and kickoffs all Tiki had to do was kick it as far as he could. He could forget all about accuracy.

Tiki felt good about that. It meant he could concentrate on scoring points the way he was supposed to—with his running game.

And maybe, just maybe, he'd even get to repeat his patented fake punt.

The first time the Eagles had the ball, Coach Wheeler kept things simple. He had Cody hand Tiki the ball on first down, and bam! Tiki did the rest. He went for a gain of twelve, and two plays later he ran for another nineteen!

After a couple of dropped passes by the receivers, Tiki got the ball again—and this time he sprinted right through a huge Paco-shaped hole in the line for a gain of twenty-three, all the way to the Badgers' twenty yard line!

Two more incompletions later it was obvious that Cody was having a tough time passing. It was a cold day—the first really cold day of the season—and the Eagles' QB seemed to be having trouble gripping the ball.

The next play was a draw play featuring John Berra, who bulled his way for eight yards.

Now it was fourth down and two to go from the twelve. A perfect field goal situation. Except, of course, that the Eagles were not *doing* that today. Instead they went for the first down. Tiki took a handoff around the end, cut the corner with amazing speed, and raced down the sideline into the end zone!

The two-point conversion was another pass to Joey Gallagher that fell short. But that was okay, Tiki told himself. They were still up by six, and they'd started the game off on the right foot.

Three minutes later that lead was gone, as the Badgers came out firing bullets after Tiki's short kick. Their quarterback, unlike Cody, seemed not to be having any problem at all with the cold weather.

So the Eagles started their next drive behind by a point, 7–6. Tiki knew he wasn't the only one on the Eagles who was on the verge of panic.

On this drive the Badgers were looking for him. Word

had obviously spread around the league that Tiki Barber was somebody you needed to double-team.

But that didn't stop Tiki. In his mind he was running for his life. No matter what happened, or how many players covered him, they weren't going to take him down.

Taking Cody's handoff, he followed Paco through the hole and into the backfield, bouncing off would-be tacklers one after the other. He was finally pushed out of bounds at the Badgers' forty-six, after a gain of thirty-five brutal yards.

After a short breather on the sidelines Tiki came back into the game. This time Cody found him on a quick dump pass, and Tiki took it from there. Jigging and jagging, zigging and zagging, he even jumped over a fallen player or two, and finally danced into the end zone, letting out a roar of triumph!

Inspired, the Eagles converted the two extra points, and took a 14–7 lead.

Tiki boomed his next kickoff—the farthest he'd kicked a ball yet—but it didn't have much height, and the returner had time to get behind his blocking and run it back all the way to the Eagles' twenty-five!

The defense held strong, thank goodness. But the Badgers did manage to notch a field goal, tightening the score to 14–10.

"Hey!" Ronde shouted at Tiki, who was moping on the bench. "Forget it, man! Just get us another touchdown!"

Tiki nodded, forcing himself to concentrate and not feel sorry for himself—at least not while the game was on.

During the next offensive series he took a screen pass from Cody on second down and ran it for a big gainer to the forty-five yard line. Then, on first down, he zipped through the line again for a quick twenty yard gain.

"Miami, baby!" Cody told the huddled team. A flea-flicker, called by Coach Wheeler.

Tiki took the handoff, then lateraled back to Cody, who hurled it over the defenders' heads to Fred Soule in the back of the end zone!

On the two-point conversion, Cody bootlegged and ran it in himself, behind a block from Tiki that put the defender flat on his behind.

"Nice blocking, little dude!" Cody said, slapping Tiki on the helmet.

Tiki usually hated it when people called attention to his size. He and Ronde were getting bigger every month, but they were still two of the shortest, skinniest kids on the team.

But right then, he was so glad to be winning—*and not kicking*—that he laughed along with Cody as they headed into the locker room for halftime.

The second half was a defensive battle, and several times it looked like the Badgers might break through for a touchdown that would make the game dangerously close.

But the Eagles' defense made a heroic goal line stand

on one drive, and on the other, Ronde made an incredible interception to prevent a sure touchdown.

The Badgers' field goal that followed made it 22–13, Eagles, and another one in the fourth quarter brought the Badgers to within a touchdown at 22–16.

There were still five minutes left to play in the game when the Eagles got the ball back at their own thirty yard line. The Badgers might have been out of the play-offs themselves, but they sure were "playing proud," Tiki thought.

They were keying on him ferociously now, and the Eagles had to go to John Berra to try to eat up the clock. But he didn't get very far, and when the two-minute warning sounded, it was fourth down and seven, with the Eagles stalled at the Badgers' forty-three.

Tiki got ready to punt. Then, looking over at the sideline, he saw Coach Wheeler flashing him the high sign.

Yesss! A fake punt! He'd almost forgotten about their secret agreement!

Tiki lined up as if to kick. He took the snap. He faked kicking—then took off almost straight ahead, zipping right past the onrushing Badgers and into the open field!

Tiki pumped his legs relentlessly forward. He was hit full force by a flying Badgers safety, but somehow he managed to hold on to the ball as he fell to the turf.

Cody grabbed his hand and yanked him up. "Dude, you okay?" The smile on his face told Tiki everything he needed to know. They'd gotten the first down they needed—the ball was still in their possession!

"Where are we?" he asked.

"Their sixteen!" Cody told him. "You sure you're okay?"

"Just give me the ball again, man," Tiki said, shaking the cobwebs out of his head.

Cody did, and Tiki put a spin move on the first Badger to come at him. He took a stagger step to avoid the second. Then he got behind a block from John Berra and took off for pay dirt.

When he crossed the goal line, he spiked the ball, fell to his knees, and let the tears flow. All the way back to the sidelines, his teammates mobbed him, hugging him and smacking him on the back and the helmet.

After another successful two-point conversion and, finally, a meaningless last-second touchdown and two-point conversion for the Badgers, the final score was 30–24, Eagles.

They were now 8–3 with one game left to go in the season. At least they hadn't knocked themselves out of play-off contention, Tiki thought with a sigh of relief.

But not *total* relief—not by a long shot.

If the teams ahead of them won their games today, the Eagles' season would be over in spite of their victory.

Well, thought Tiki, *I guess all we can do now is wait.*

CHAPTER NINE

THE SLIM THREAD OF HOPE

THE BOYS WERE EATING THE DINNER THEIR MOM had prepared for them—stuffed shells and salad, with cupcakes for dessert.

The note she'd left said, *I know you boys made me proud today, even though I couldn't be there. And when you play proud and live proud, win or lose, good things are bound to happen.*

Ronde and Tiki both knew what she meant. It wasn't the kind of proud where you strut around bragging about yourself. Living proud meant acting in a way that made you proud of yourself. It meant doing the right thing, even when no one was looking.

The phone rang, bringing Ronde's thoughts back to the moment. "You answer it," he said, his mouth full of food. "I'm still eating."

Tiki's eyes went wide. "And what am *I* doing? Sitting here watching you eat? I'm not your secretary."

"How do you know it's for me? It's probably for mom, or else it's one of those sales calls."

All this time, while they were arguing, the phone kept on ringing.

Tiki finally pushed his plate away and went to answer it. "You owe me for this," he told Ronde. "Hello?"

The voice on the other end was Paco's, Ronde could tell. He was yelling that loud.

"Whoa, dude, hold up! Slow down so I can understand you!" Tiki said. As he listened, his eyes went wide, and a big grin spread across his face. "Yeah, man! Oh, baby, yeah!"

"What? What!"

Tiki waved Ronde off. "Dude, we'll be right over." He hung up and clapped his hands. "Come on, Ronde. We're going over to Paco's to celebrate."

"What happened?" Ronde asked.

"The Colts and the Bears lost!"

"Both of them?"

"Yup—and to really weak teams too! Ronde, man, we're still alive! Can you believe it? We're still breathing!"

"Woo-hoo!"

At Paco's they got all the details. "My friend Stewie Brewer was over there at the Bears game? His cousin goes there or something. So he calls me after, 'cause he knows I'm dying over here, and he says the Bears got wiped out by the Mountaineers, twenty to zero, or something like that!"

"And how'd you hear about the Colts game?" Ronde wondered.

"My cousin works for the *Roanoke Reporter* in their mail room. So I called him and he found out for me. Close game. Twenty-four to seventeen, Panthers."

"Wow," Ronde said, shaking his head. "Did we get lucky today or what?"

"Imagine *both* those games ending in upsets," Tiki said. "But, man, am I glad they did!"

"Well, don't get too excited," Ronde warned. "Lightning has to strike again next week. *And*, by the way, we also have to *win*."

"Hey," Ronde said. "You know what? I just thought of something. If we win next week and the Colts and the Bears lose, we're all tied in the standings, right?"

"Yeah . . . so?"

"Well, the tiebreaker is the teams' record against each other—and we beat the Colts twice and split two with the Bears. But we outscored them, and that's the tiebreaker. If we win and either of them loses, we're in!"

"Hey, he's right!" Paco said brightly. Then his expression darkened. "But you left out one thing. We're playing the Rockets. They're nine–two so far."

"Hey, Paco," Ronde said, "just remember, one of those losses was against us."

Paco tilted his head to the side. "I don't know, guys," he said. "We had Adam in that game, remember. He made a big difference, and we won by three points."

He blew out a breath, and looked up at the twins. "So . . . are we going to have him back for this game, or what?"

"He takes his math makeup test tomorrow," Ronde said. "If he passes, he can take the biology makeup next Wednesday. And if he passes that one too, he can play on Thursday."

"Whoa," Paco said nervously. "I sure hope you guys are getting through to him."

"Keep your fingers crossed," Tiki told him.

"Hey, Paco," Ronde said, "look at the bright side. There's only one team we have to catch now."

"Yeah, but the Colts are playing the Panthers, the Bears are up against the Mountaineers, and we're playing the Rockets. That's not a good situation. You two guys had better get Adam in shape, or I don't like our odds."

The next day at practice everyone was nervous. They all knew that Adam was inside, taking his math makeup test.

Ronde kept sneaking looks at the doorway. He knew that when the test was done, Adam would come through those doors. And in an instant, by the look on his face, the whole team would know their fate.

"Hey, Ronde, wake up!"

Ronde snapped back to attention at the sound of Coach Wheeler's voice. It was hard to concentrate, he had to admit. And yet he had to. The upcoming game was the most important one of their entire season. If they won, they at least had a fighting chance. If they lost, it was all over, no matter what the other teams did.

Still, every one of the Eagles knew that their chances against a good team like the North Side Rockets were much better with a great kicker on their side.

And a great kicker, Tiki was not.

The practice was tense, and the players were making way more mistakes than usual. Everyone, it seemed, was having a hard time concentrating. Their minds were all on Adam, and their eyes were all sneaking constant looks at those doors.

Ronde thought back to that last tutoring session he'd had with Adam. He sure hoped Adam had absorbed the football comparison. If he failed his makeup test, not only would it be devastating for the Eagles, but it would be personally embarrassing for Ronde.

Finally, after what seemed like hours, the fateful doors swung open. There stood Adam Costa, a blank expression on his face. He looked them over—all his fifty-seven teammates—and then he smiled and flashed the team a big thumbs-up!

A cheer went up from every corner of the football field. Adam had not only passed his math test, but he'd gotten a B!

Hope was still alive!

CHAPTER TEN
LIFE LESSONS

TIKI SAT AT THE TABLE, HIS CHIN IN HIS HANDS, staring glumly across at Adam. He wished he could be at practice right now, busting a run or catching a screen pass.

But no—he had to spend the entire afternoon helping someone else do his homework—and then spend the entire evening doing his own!

He felt sorry for Adam, sure. Who wouldn't? Tiki stared across at his old friend as he scratched his head, squinted his eyes, and pressed so hard on his pencil that he broke the tip for the hundredth time in the past hour.

"I just can't get this stuff through my thick skull!" Adam complained, banging his head with his fist for emphasis. "I am so dumb!"

"Cut it out, will you?" Tiki begged, rolling his eyes. "We both know you're not dumb. Remember back in seventh grade chemistry, when you memorized all the elements?"

"That was different," Adam explained. "I just learned the lyrics to this old song my dad turned me on to, 'The

Elements.' All I had to do was say the words out loud and leave out the tune."

Tiki shook his head and laughed. "Well, if you could do that, why can't you do *this*?"

"There's no song that lists the parts of a cell."

"So? Make one up!"

"You think I can just make up a tune in my head?"

Hmm. Maybe not, thought Tiki. He'd have to find another way to get Adam over his mental block.

But it was hard to think of good ideas when all he could keep his mind on was football practice, where all the rest of their teammates were getting ready for the huge game on Thursday night.

What if all this time he was spending with Adam turned out to be wasted? What if Adam failed his makeup test on Wednesday and Tiki had to be the kicker in that critical, final game of the season?

He'd gotten by against the lowly Panthers, but the Rockets were a different story. They were already headed for the play-offs.

That was the Eagles' best hope—that the game wasn't really important to North Side. But Tiki knew that if it was *him*, being in the play-offs wouldn't matter. He always wanted to crush *every* opponent—and he was pretty sure the Rockets felt the same way.

"Hey, are you paying attention?" Adam said.

Tiki snapped out of his reverie. "Uh, sure I am."

"Yeah? What'd I just say?"

"Uh . . . Okay, okay, I was daydreaming. Sorry."

"We don't have much time, Tiki. I need you to focus!"

"*You* need *me* to focus?"

"Yes! Come on, man. I've got to get myself back on the team, and fast!"

Adam was right. Tiki was angry at himself now. He should have realized no one felt worse about the Eagles' troubles than Adam, who was most responsible for them.

"Okay, okay, I'm focusing," he said. "Let's get back to work."

That night he and Ronde lay in their beds in the dark. Tiki couldn't sleep. He kept staring at the ceiling, where he could see the shadows of leaves cast by the moonlight. They danced back and forth, keeping him awake, the thoughts dancing in his head to the same beat.

"Ronde? You awake?"

"Uh-huh," came the answer.

"I can't sleep."

"Me neither."

"Adam's gonna fail this biology makeup test."

"He is?"

"Yeah, man. I'm a lousy tutor."

"Huh."

"Maybe you could take over? You did a good job with the math makeup."

"Yeah, but you know you're better than me at science."

"True," Tiki admitted. "But maybe you're a better teacher."

"Nah, that's not it, Tiki. You've just got to find some way to get through to Adam. I had the same problem with him—he just couldn't get it about equations."

"So what did you do?"

"I used football stuff as an example."

"Hmm . . ."

"Anyway, don't give up. Adam's not as dumb as he looks."

"Ha!"

"No, seriously, man. Try to think of a football comparison that works, and he'll get it, because that's what his mind's really zoned in on."

Of course! How could Tiki not have seen it? If he had been sitting there with Adam thinking about football, how could Adam not have been thinking about it too?

"Thanks, Ronde. I think I'll try that. Yeah . . . that's what I'm gonna do . . ."

"Oh, and one more thing," said Ronde. "Adam's really down on himself these days."

"Yeah, I noticed."

"So you've got to find a way to make him feel smart.

You know, like he can pass that test, no problem."

"Right."

Tiki stared again at the leaf shadows dancing on the ceiling. Adam needed confidence, he could see that—but so did *he*! He'd never tried to be a teacher before, and he'd never really tried kicking, either.

Tiki knew he needed a little help at both.

"Man, I don't know if this is working," Adam said.

"One more time," Tiki begged. "Name me the parts of a cell."

Adam groaned and pounded his head with both fists. "I need a break from all this pressure!"

"Okay, okay," Tiki said, backing off. "Let's go outside and throw the football around for a while."

Adam brightened up instantly. "Now you're talking. Come on!" He got up, grabbed a football off the floor, and led Tiki downstairs.

"Where do you think you're going?" Adam's mother asked them as they headed for the backyard.

"We're taking a break," Tiki explained. "We both need it."

"Just for ten minutes," Adam said.

His mom frowned. "How's it going up there?"

"Good!" Tiki rushed to reply. "Really good, Mrs. Costa."

"Hmmm. Well, all right, then. But just for ten minutes."

The two boys tossed the ball around a few times, pretending to make awesome catches, falling from invisible tackles, laughing and working up a good sweat.

"Hey, Adam," Tiki said after a few minutes. "Before we go back inside, I need you to help me with my kicking. You know . . . just in case."

Adam flinched. "In case I flunk my makeup test, you mean?" he asked.

"Well . . . to be honest, yeah," Tiki admitted. "I stink at kicking, and if you're not there, I can't afford to stink."

"Okay," Adam agreed. "Let's see you placekick a few times."

There was a field hockey net set up in the Costas' backyard. Adam knelt down and held the football so that Tiki could kick it into the net.

"Good!" Adam said after Tiki whacked his first attempt straight into the net. "Excellent!" he said after Tiki nailed the second.

Tiki tried about half a dozen kicks, and most of them were struck perfectly. "I don't know what you think your problem is," Adam said, shrugging. "You're fine at kicking."

"Nuh-uh," Tiki said. "Not when it's in a real game. I freeze right up—especially with all those dudes in the other uniforms rushing at me."

"Huh."

"I don't know how you do it, man."

"Wanna know the secret?" Adam said, flashing a grin. "I just get into this zone—this quiet place inside my head, see? Nobody can come in, no noise can penetrate. It's just me, my foot, and the ball."

"Wow," Tiki said softly. "Cool. Sure hope I don't have to try doing that Thursday."

"You and me both."

"ADAM!" His mother shouted from inside the house. "Ten minutes are up!"

"Okay, okay!" He sighed. Then he noticed that Tiki was suddenly lost in thought. "Uh, Tiki? What's wrong?"

"Nothing, man—nothing's wrong. I just got an idea, that's all."

"An idea?"

"Yeah, about the parts of a cell."

"Oh, that."

"ADAM!"

"COMING, MA!" He turned to Tiki. "Can you tell me inside?"

"Sure, man. Sure."

They went back up to Adam's room and sat down at his desk. "Okay, here it is," Tiki said. "You ready?"

"Sure. Shoot."

"Okay. Now, think of the cell as a football field."

"What?"

"Just go with me on this, dude. Zone in, like you do when you're gonna make a kick."

"Okay. I'm zoning. Go on."

"So the cell is the whole field. The head coach is the nucleus, okay? 'Cause he runs the whole game, and tells all the players what to do."

"Ha! I get it. That's pretty cool. But what about the other parts?"

"Well, the vacuoles? They're like the watercoolers, because they keep everything hydrated."

"Funny!"

"Stay focused now. The lysosomes, they're the defense."

"Because they break things down, like tackling!"

"Exactly!"

"What about the mitochondria?"

"Well, they power the cell, right?"

"Yeah . . ."

"So, they're like the cheerleaders."

"Awesome!"

"And the yard lines that divide up the field?"

"Let me think . . . The endoplasmic reticulum?"

"Right! Because it divides up the parts of the cell!"

"This is so cool!" Adam said, slapping Tiki five. "Just like learning that song about the elements!"

"Come on. We're not done yet," Tiki said impatiently. "The ribosomes?"

"Uh . . . let's see . . . They build muscles, so . . . the weight room?"

"That's right! And the cell membrane?"

"The sidelines!"

"Great! Now let's go over the whole thing again, okay?"

"No problem, Tiki. You know, suddenly it all seems so obvious. I actually think we're gonna nail this thing!"

Tiki walked back home from Adam's feeling more hopeful than he had in a long time. On the way he ran into Joey Gallagher, who was riding his bike home.

"Hey, Barber! Where were you?"

"Working with Adam on his science homework," Tiki explained.

"That's nice," Joey said. "But you know he's never gonna get cleared for the game. We needed you out there today, practicing with the whole team. North Side is no pushover, Tiki. We've all got to pull together if we're going to beat them."

"Yeah, I know," Tiki replied. "But, Joey, sometimes you've gotta take care of business *off* the field before you can take care of business *on* it."

"Whatever," said Joey, giving himself a kick start and wobbling off down the street on his bike.

"And Adam's going to play Thursday!" Tiki shouted after him. "I guarantee it!"

CHAPTER ELEVEN

THREADING THE NEEDLE

WEDNESDAY AFTERNOON, AT THE START OF THEIR
final practice of the regular season, Coach Wheeler gathered the team together in the locker room.

"I wanted to talk to you all before tomorrow's game,"
he said. He cleared his throat and looked them over.

Ronde did the same. He saw the rapt faces of fifty-six
boys his own age, all in uniform, all united in a single
purpose—winning a football game and making the
play-offs.

"Tomorrow we face the North Side Rockets," Coach
Wheeler went on. "They're a strong squad, and as we
already know, they can play tough, especially on defense.
Their linebackers are strong and fast, and we especially
need to look out for their free safety. He really punished
us last time we played them."

Coach Wheeler's steely gaze fixed itself on them all,
one after another. "Last time we played, it was our fourth
game of the season, and we won by the skin of our teeth.
I'm sure you all remember that game very well."

He paused for a long moment, letting the players

remember how Cody, their quarterback, had been picked off repeatedly and in the end had been benched for a substitute.

Still, they'd won the game, and it was because most of them had studied videotape of the Rockets' other games. In a way it was Coach Wheeler who'd won that game for the Eagles and had kept them in the play-off hunt.

"As for North Side, it was their first defeat," the coach said. "After they faced us, they put in a new quarterback and proceeded to go on a long winning streak. As you saw yesterday when we watched the videotape, he's a scrambler. So Ronde and Reeves, you two are going to have to stay ready, in case he runs the option and rolls out.

"And another thing," Wheeler went on. "Their coach is terrific at getting their guys to make adjustments. So we're going to have to change our game plan midgame, before they can react."

He cleared his throat again. "Which will be easy, because I can't really make a complete game plan anyway—not until we know if we've got Costa back."

He glanced quickly from side to side, to see how the team was reacting to his words. Ronde noticed that although no one said anything, they all looked at one another—and at Tiki.

Poor Tiki, thought Ronde. *I sure am glad Coach didn't make me the new kicker!*

"Adam's taking his biology makeup test this afternoon,

so we should know by the end of practice whether we've got him back or not. In the meantime we're going to do some no-contact scrimmaging. And, Cody, I want you to give our defense a little practice with a scrambling QB." He smiled. "Just for fun, okay?"

Cody grinned and nodded. "Sure thing, Coach."

Ronde knew that the coach and the quarterback had become close this season, after the rockiest of beginnings. Cody was different now—more of a humble team player. But Coach Wheeler had changed too. He was much more forceful now, more inspiring and positive.

"We've beaten the Rockets once," Wheeler concluded, "and we can do it again, if we play the way we know how to."

"Proud," Ronde said.

"What's that, Ronde?" Coach Wheeler asked.

"We've got to play proud. That's what my mom always says."

Coach Wheeler smiled. "Hear that, team? Let's win one for Mrs. Barber, okay?"

A roar went up from the Eagles, and they smacked one another on the helmets as they ran out onto the field.

Well, thought Ronde, *it's all fine and good to play proud. But if Adam fails his makeup test, we're still in a heap of trouble.*

After a few minutes it was clear that Ronde wasn't the only one whose mind was on something besides football.

Players kept dropping passes, blowing coverages, missing blocks and tackles. And Tiki's kicks were the worst they'd ever been.

It was toward the end of the session—almost five o'clock—when Adam finally emerged from the double steel doors onto the playing field.

Everyone stopped what they were doing. Ronde, who was about to intercept a pass, let the ball hit him in the head because he'd stopped watching it. Luckily, nobody noticed. All eyes were on Adam Costa.

Adam was looking glumly at the ground, and Ronde could feel a big lump growing in his own throat.

Could it be? Had Adam failed yet again? Were the Eagles doomed to play their final game without him?

Adam looked up—looked at all of them, slowly spanning the field from left to right—and then he broke into a mile-wide grin, raised his fists, and nodded.

"YESSSSS!" Ronde screamed. So did all the others, jumping up and down and hugging whoever was nearby. Then they all made a beeline for Adam.

"WHOA!" Adam yelled, holding his hands out to fend them off. "Don't hurt me, please! I bruise easily!"

Instead of tackling him, they hoisted him on their shoulders and ran him all the way back to the locker room.

The Eagles were united again—finally! Now, thought Ronde, they could go into tomorrow's game with confidence.

Watch out, North Side, he told himself. *Here come the real Hidden Valley Eagles!*

Of course, it might not matter, he had to remind himself. The Eagles could pulverize the Rockets and still not make the play-offs. As of today there were still four teams in the conference with better records than they had.

In first place were the Pulaski Wildcats, with a record of 10–1. But that 1 represented a loss to the Eagles, 38–3! That had been early in the season, Ronde remembered, when they'd first gotten it together as a team.

"I hope we get to play them again in the play-offs," he told Tiki as they sat doing their homework Thursday afternoon.

"Me too," Tiki said. "I hope we get to play *anybody.*"

It had been a weird day, in a way. Their game against the Rockets wasn't scheduled to start till seven p.m. So instead of just heading for the locker room after school to suit up for their usual afternoon game, they'd gone home and worked on their homework and polished off an early dinner their mom had left for them in the fridge.

Because of the weird scheduling Tiki and Ronde both kept looking at the clock, realizing that they'd know before the game started whether they still had a chance at making the play-offs.

Only four teams would get there. The Wildcats were already in. So were the North Side Rockets, in second place with a 9–2 record. Yet the Eagles had beaten them, too—and might do it again tonight.

If they did, that would give the two teams an identical 9–3 record, but the Eagles would finish higher because they'd have beaten the Rockets twice head-on.

There were two other teams that had 9–2 records. One was the Martinsville Colts—and guess what? The Eagles had beaten them twice too. That meant if the Colts lost and the Eagles won, they'd both be 9–3, but the Eagles would finish ahead, again because of their head-on record.

The fourth team ahead of the Eagles, also at 9–2, was the Blue Ridge Bears. The Eagles had played the Bears twice, and had split the two games. But as all the Eagles knew, the next tiebreaker after the head-on record was the margin of victory.

Here too the Eagles had the advantage. They'd lost by a single point in one of the games, and had won the other by twenty points.

The bottom line was, if both the Bears and the Colts lost today and the Eagles won, the Eagles were in. But if both the Bears and Colts won, *or* if the Eagles lost, it was all over. They would finish fifth, and out of the running.

"Would you stop tapping your pencil?" Tiki begged. "You're driving me crazy."

"Sorry. I was just figuring out the possibilities of us getting into the play-offs."

"You don't have to be a math genius to figure that one out."

"Okay, so what are the odds?" Ronde challenged him.

"Huh?"

"You know—the percentages?"

"How should I know?"

Ronde laughed. "You'd *better* know, man. We don't want you getting suspended from the team like you-know-who."

Soon Ronde found himself getting annoyed with Tiki—who was tapping his pencil exactly like Ronde had before.

"Cut that out!" said Ronde.

"Sorry." Tiki looked up at the clock on the wall. "Should be anytime now."

It was after five o'clock. The afternoon games would be ending any minute. Paco's spies would call him on the phone, as usual. And then they'd hear from Paco.

Ronde sure hoped the call would come before they had to leave for school. He figured they had about five minutes before their mom showed up from work to drive them over there in the station wagon.

RRRRing!

Both boys jumped up from the kitchen table so fast that they flipped their chairs over backward. Ronde ran for the living room extension, and Tiki lunged for the kitchen phone.

"Hello?" they both yelled at once.

"It's a miracle!" Paco shouted back. "Can you believe it? They both lost!"

Ronde let out a whoop and started jumping up and down. Finally he heard Tiki yell, "Quiet down, yo! I want to hear what Paco has to say!"

"So?" Ronde said, back into the receiver. "What happened?"

"The Bears fumbled five times in the second half!" Paco explained. "They lost twenty-one to fourteen. And the Colts lost seven to zero—nobody could move the ball. Everybody just kept slipping and falling!"

"Huh?" Ronde said.

"Dude, have you looked out the window at all in the past hour?" Paco asked. "Check it out, and you'll see why. Gotta go, yo. See you at the field. We win, we're in!"

More whooping, and both Barber boys hung up. Ronde beat Tiki to the window, and drew aside the shade.

"Whoa."

Outside it was snowing. Big, fat flakes that were turning to slush in the street and in the driveway. "Slippery going today, Tiki."

"Yeah," Tiki agreed as they saw their mom's station wagon pull into the driveway and heard the horn honk. "Okay, man. Let's go get this game."

They slapped five, grabbed their coats, and headed out the door, into the snow, ready for the Eagles' date with destiny.

CHAPTER TWELVE

THE GAME OF THEIR LIVES

IT HAD STARTED OUT AS RAIN, AT ABOUT TWO THAT afternoon. By five, when Tiki and Ronde had gotten the call from Paco, the rain had turned to snow—big, fat flakes that turned to slush and splattered all over you when you walked.

Now it was six fifteen, and the snow was changing over to sleet. Tiki knew that the ball would be as slippery and cold as an ice cube.

As they ran into the locker room and out of the storm, Ronde shouted, "Man, this weather stinks! Why does everything have to be so hard on us?"

"Don't complain," Tiki told him. "It'll be just as hard on the other team. Hey, Ronde, we've come this far. We can't let a little bad weather stop us now."

"You're right, Tiki. No complaining tonight. If we win, we're in. If we lose . . ."

"Then we've got only ourselves to blame," Tiki finished for him.

Still, Tiki knew that the bad weather would make it hard on both teams' passing games. That hurt the Eagles more than the Rockets, who relied mainly on their defense.

The Eagles' passing game, while it wasn't the team's biggest strength, was good enough to make the defense spread out. And that left huge holes for Tiki to run through.

But tonight there wasn't going to be any distraction. If the Eagles were going to get to the play-offs, Tiki knew, they were going to have to pound their way in with the running game, past a stiff Rockets defense that was expecting them to do just that.

Tiki was relieved that he wouldn't have to do the kicking tonight. That would have doomed the team for sure.

In the locker room everyone was excited. The talk was all about their huge good fortune, with both the Bears and the Colts losing two weeks in a row.

"We're getting in through the back door," Cody said, "But who cares? Once we're in, we're the team to beat."

"That's right," said Sam Scarfone, who always agreed with Cody. "We've beaten all those other teams, and they know it—we'll be in their heads!"

"Would you just chill out?" Tiki said. "Let's get ourselves into the play-offs before we start thinking we're all that and a bag of chips."

"Sorry," Cody said, putting up both hands. "When you're right, you're right. Let's go get us a win, then."

A cheer went up from the players, and right on cue Coach Wheeler made his entrance.

"Thank you, thank you," he said, bowing to laughter and applause. Instantly Tiki felt the mood in the locker room lighten up and the players relax.

That was good, he thought. *They needed to play loose tonight.*

"Okay, troops," Coach Wheeler said, gathering the team for his pregame speech. "This is it. This is the big one. We've worked our hardest to get this far, and I'm proud of each and every one of you. I expect to be even prouder when this game's over."

"He sounds just like Mom," Ronde whispered to Tiki.

Tiki grinned and nodded, and he and Ronde exchanged their secret ritual handshake.

"We're going to run at them," Coach Wheeler explained. "That's because it's a slick field out there. Ball handlers, beware. The team that fumbles the most tonight is the team that loses. Let's not have it be us.

"Grab that ball with both hands and keep it in tight. Don't be trying for that extra half yard at the end of the play, because somebody's going to hit you, and the ball's going to come loose. Just go down when you're tackled, and *hold on to the ball.*"

Tiki knew Coach was talking to him and Ronde more than anyone else—Tiki did 75 percent of the team's running, and Ronde ran back the kickoffs and punts.

"Now, let's get out there and shoot down the Rockets!"

The Eagles went into their team chant, ending up in a loud roar as they ran through the doors and out onto Hidden Valley field.

The home crowd went wild. Tiki was surprised to see how full the stands were, considering the miserable weather. He knew his mom was out there—she never missed a home game, work or no work—but the rest of the huge crowd?

Tiki felt really good inside that the Hidden Valley students and parents were so fully behind their team. Even the principal was there—Dr. Anand was in the front row of the bleachers, cheering and clapping with all the rest of them!

Of course, there was even more pressure to win when you were playing at home, with everyone you knew watching.

Tiki forced himself to shut out all such thoughts. He hoped his teammates were doing the same, because it wasn't just the team with fewer fumbles that would win tonight—it was the team that came with the better mental game.

Tiki glanced over at Adam as he practiced kicking into the old soccer net. Joey, doing the holding, kept saying "Ouch!" on every kick.

Tiki knew that with the cold air and the hard, frozen ball, the vibrations must have been going right through Joey's hands.

The Eagles lost the coin toss. Not a bad thing on a night like tonight, Tiki thought—a night when most of the points were likely to come from the defenses of both teams pouncing on mistakes.

Tiki wondered how Adam's leg would respond to the long layoff—but he needn't have worried. Adam's first kickoff was low, but plenty long enough.

Tiki didn't know if he'd kicked it that way on purpose, but it sure came out well, because the ball was bouncing and sliding around all over the place. After a furious free-for-all, the Rockets covered it way back on their own three yard line!

Everyone slapped Adam on the helmet and shouted, "Great kick!" and "Good to have you back, man!" and "That's our kicker!"

Wow, Tiki thought. *Adam must feel like a million bucks right now.* He just hoped he would feel the same way when the game was over.

The Rockets ran the ball three times but couldn't get any farther than the nine yard line. Their punter barely got the ball away, and only a lucky bounce saved them from disaster. The ball rolled all the way up to the Rockets' forty-five before Ronde smothered it.

Tiki felt good about the Eagles' chances as he snapped

his chin strap on. Good field position, and the Rockets were already looking shaky.

On first down Cody gave him the ball, and Paco totally nailed his man, allowing Tiki to run straight ahead through the line.

For a second he thought he saw daylight all the way to the end zone. But the Rockets' linebacker hit him from the blind side and threw him to the ground. It was all Tiki could do to hold on to the ball.

Wow, he thought. *It's even worse out here than I thought!*

Next down it was John Berra's turn. He managed to push the pile far enough forward for a first down at the thirty-four.

Tiki's turn again. But this time there was no hole in the middle. He had to run it around the side, and when he tried to cut and turn upfield, his feet slipped right out from under him. He landed hard, and slid all the way off the field and into the crowd of Rockets standing on their sideline.

"WHOA!" they all shouted, laughing.

Tiki got up and ran back onto the field. Behind him he heard one of them shouting, "Learn to skate, kid!"

Cody tried a quarterback draw on the next down, but he was thrown for a loss of five when John Berra's man faked him out and went right by the attempted block.

On third down the Eagles went to Tiki again. This

time the Rockets were there even before he got to the hole, and they threw him for a three yard loss.

Time to punt, and Tiki ran off the field, disappointed. He was glad it wasn't him who had to punt, though.

Adam's kick took an Eagles bounce and went into the end zone for a touchback, giving the Rockets the ball at their own twenty. Not great field position, but better than it could have been.

The game soon turned into a slushfest, with icing on top. The field was like a skating rink. As the teams slogged back and forth through the first two quarters, it was pretty much a battle of field position—a battle the Eagles were winning, but without putting any points on the board.

Tiki was getting more and more tense, and from the looks on the other Eagles' faces, he wasn't alone. He had the creepy feeling that the first team to score would be the winner of this game—and that the first team to cough up the ball would be the loser.

Finally, with only one minute left in the half, the Eagles got the break they were looking for. The Rockets' coach must have been getting frustrated with his team going nowhere, because he took a big gamble and had his quarterback throw long, going for the big score.

Tiki looked down the field and saw, to his horror, that Ronde had fallen down! The receiver was all alone, and waving his hands for the quarterback to throw him the ball.

But the quarterback didn't *have* the ball—it had slipped out of his hand when he'd reared back to throw it! And now it was flying through the air, with at least six players leaping for it!

It looked more like a game of volleyball than football, but the main thing was that Sam Scarfone—never known for his hands, but at least they were enormous—came down with the ball and lumbered all the way to the Rockets' six yard line!

Tiki yelled and jumped for joy. He promised himself that the very next time he took the ball, he was going to score a touchdown.

On first down he took the handoff and started to one side, waiting for a hole to open up in the line. When he saw it, he didn't waste a second.

Tucking the ball in tight like Coach had told him to do, he lowered his head and bulled his way forward, letting himself bounce off tackle after tackle. Covered with mud as he was, no one could get a firm grip on him, and he ended the play with a dive into the end zone that sent slush and mud splattering everywhere!

The Eagles and their fans went wild. There was dancing in the bleachers, and the school's marching band played a happy tune.

After making the extra point look easy, Adam sent the kickoff out of the end zone for another touchback. Ten seconds later the half ended with the Eagles up, 7–0.

Tiki and the rest of the team couldn't get into the locker room fast enough.

"Man, it is *cold* out there!" someone said.

"Brrrrr!" someone else agreed.

"Somebody jack up the heat!"

Coach Wheeler told them to stay focused. "They're bringing out the snowplow to clear the field, so it should be a little better out there, at least for the first few minutes of the second half. And since we get the ball first, let's try a few quick passes. Let's go to Tiki in the flat, and then try a screen."

He looked at Tiki with those penetrating eagle eyes of his. "I'm trusting you to make the catch before you start running—and to hold on to the ball," he said, grabbing Tiki by the arm. "*Hold on to it, no matter what.* Understand?"

"Yes, Coach," Tiki said, nodding. "I'll try."

"No—don't *try*. Trying is not good enough. Trying means you've defeated yourself before you've even begun. Don't try—*do*."

"Y-yes, Coach. I'll catch it, and I'll keep it."

"Good. That's what I want to hear. Everybody, on those first two plays keep the Rockets away from Tiki. Got it?"

"YES, COACH!"

"Okay. Let's get back out there!"

A cheer went up from the players, and they ran back onto the field chanting, "EA-GLES! EA-GLES!"

Ronde received the kickoff, and instead of just covering the ball and falling to the ground to protect it, he started running upfield.

He must see a lane, Tiki thought. "Go, Ronde!" he shouted along with everybody else.

Ronde made it all the way out to the forty yard line. A good start to the second half.

Now it was Tiki's turn. Cody faked a handoff to John Berra, then dropped back. He faked a long bomb, just to throw off the rushers. Then he turned and found Tiki at the forty-seven.

Tiki caught the ball, making sure to take it in with soft hands—absorbing it, the way a trampoline absorbs a jumper's impact. Expecting to get hit any second, he did a blind spin move to his right and found, to his surprise, that he had an open field ahead of him!

The footing was still slippery but not as bad as before the half. Tiki couldn't really make many moves, so he just barreled forward until he was brought down by the safety at the Rockets' forty-two.

First down, Eagles!

Next was the screen pass, and it was a beauty. Tiki took it and watched the wall of blockers form ahead of him. He followed their lead all the way down to the thirty-three yard line!

Second and one, and Cody dove for the first down. The Eagles were now set up for another score. But the sleet hadn't stopped falling, and already the newly plowed field was turning white again.

On the next snap Cody slipped and fell while dropping back, and was pounced on by the Rocket left tackle. The ball came loose, and one of the Rockets picked it up. Before Tiki knew what was happening, he was chasing the ballcarrier back the other way!

He finally caught him at the Eagles' fourteen, but now it was the Rockets who were on the march. Before five minutes had gone by in the third quarter, they'd scored their first TD.

Then came a play that caught all the Eagles by surprise. Tiki watched as the Rockets lined up for the extra-point kick—then faked it and ran around the end for a successful two-point conversion!

Suddenly the Eagles were trailing, 8–7, in the most important game of their lives. And with the sleet coming down, scoring was going to be hard.

Could it really be? Tiki wondered. *Are we really about to lose? Are we really going to get shut out of these play-offs?*

Ronde took the kickoff but could do nothing on the slippery turf except run it out of bounds.

The two teams proceeded to spend the rest of the second half the way they'd spent most of the first—in a seesaw scoreless tug-of-war on a field that just kept getting slicker and slicker.

With only one minute and fifty-two seconds left in

the game—and left in the Eagles' season unless things changed—Ronde made a key play that gave them all a breath of hope.

On third down and long the Rockets were forced to try a pass. Coach Wheeler knew it, and he called for an all-out blitz. Ronde was the first man through. He hit the Rockets' quarterback on the blind side, just as he was about to let the ball fly to his wide-open receiver.

The ball flew straight up into the air instead. On his back, Ronde let it come down right into his arms!

And so, incredibly, against all odds, the Eagles had one last chance to save their entire season.

Tiki ran back out onto the field, saying to himself, *Let's go! Let's do it! Right now!*

The ball was on the Rockets' twenty-one yard line. And there it stayed for three straight downs as the Eagles tried and failed to advance.

Tiki ran for no gain. So did John Berra. And on third down Cody ran a keeper around an end. He wound up fumbling, but luckily the ball went out of bounds, stopping the clock with just five seconds left!

Tiki looked over to the sideline. It was fourth down. In a normal game this would have been the time to bring out Adam for a game-winning field goal.

But in this mess?

Here came Adam anyway, with his gawky trot, clapping his hands and grinning like a fool.

Tiki did the math—if Adam could somehow keep his footing and nail this kick, it would be a field goal of thirty-seven yards.

There's no way, Tiki couldn't help thinking. Oh, sure, on a nice sunny day with no wind, Adam could probably kick it through from there, no problem. He was as good as any high school kicker in Virginia.

But not on a day like this! All Adam's kicks so far that night had been low line drives. It was really hard to get under the ball when you had to keep from slipping at the same time!

And not only that but the long snap was hard to control with a frozen ball. Not to mention the fact that Joey Gallagher would have to catch it and put down a perfect hold.

Stop worrying! Tiki told himself. *If it's meant to be, it's meant to be.*

The ball was snapped, Joey gathered it in, and Adam—good old Adam—passed the hardest test he'd taken all year. He kicked that ball, sweet and true, right through the center of the uprights!

The band struck up a victory march and the Eagles all ran out onto the field as the gun sounded to end the game. They'd done it!

Tiki went over to shake hands with some of the defeated Rockets.

"We'll get you back in the play-offs," one of them said good-naturedly.

"Yeah? We'll see," Tiki said, smiling. He was just glad that they'd still be playing football after Thanksgiving!

Tiki looked over to where the happy Eagles' linemen were hoisting Adam onto their shoulders. Tiki shook his head and laughed.

"Look at that!" he told Ronde, who'd come over to give him a big bear hug. "That Costa is one lucky dude. He could have been the goat—easy."

"Yeah," agreed Ronde with a big grin. "And you and me along with him, if he'd failed those tests. Oh, well. I guess that's how the football bounces!"

CHAPTER THIRTEEN

THE HAPPY RECAP

THEY WERE A BUNCH OF MUD-COATED FILTHY SOGGY but oh-so-happy Eagles as they slogged back into the locker room. Ronde felt almost dizzy, and he couldn't stop whooping at the top of his lungs along with all the rest of them.

Hugs were exchanged all around, as well as elaborate handshakes, high fives, low fives, and all the fives in between. Helmets butted helmets, locker doors got drummed on, and the level of noise was enough to make Ronde cover his ears.

It was almost impossible to believe. How in the world, he wondered, had the Eagles managed to sneak into the play-offs after blowing those three games?

Yet here they were. Their season was *not* over, and with any luck it might last all the way to Christmas vacation!

Coach Wheeler came in from the field, along with defensive coach Pete Pellugi and offensive coach Steve Ontkos. Everyone cheered, and started chanting, "Coach! Coach! Coach! Coach!"

Wheeler held up his hands, grinning from ear to ear. "We've come a long way, haven't we?"

"Yeah!" everyone shouted.

"And we've got a long way yet to go!"

"WOO-HOO!"

"But if we play like we *can* play, I'll tell you this right now—there's no reason we can't wind up district champions—maybe even state champs!"

"YEEEAAHHHHH!"

"So let's dare to dream, huh? Tomorrow we're back at practice, and by the way—guess who our first opponent is?"

A murmur rumbled across the locker room as they all looked at one another and shrugged.

"The same team we beat today. That's right, and they'll be looking for revenge. So let's not give it to them, huh?"

"Whoooooo!" came the deafening reply.

"One more thing before I let you go get cleaned up," said the coach. "First I want to thank Coach Pellugi and Coach Ontkos. You guys are the best!"

"Coach! Coach! Coach!" came the chant, accompanied by applause.

"And now for today's game ball. It goes to none other than our long-lost kicker, Adam Costa!"

The loudest cheer yet went up as Adam came up to accept his muddy, frozen football.

"Costa, you finally passed a test!" Paco teased, and everyone laughed.

"Thank you, thank you," Adam said, flashing his goofy grin. "But I have to say, this really belongs to Tiki and Ronde, because without their help with my studying, I wouldn't have even been here today."

That caught Ronde totally by surprise. He felt his face flush as everyone turned to him and Tiki, and started chanting "Bar-ber! Bar-ber!"

But he knew it was true. Without the help he and his twin had given their friend in his time of need, the whole team would have suffered.

What do you know? he thought. *Coach was right. Football really is a mental game.*

Ronde and Tiki rode home in the station wagon with their mom, who'd been waiting patiently for them to clean up and finish their locker room celebration.

"I've got a special surprise for you two at home," she said with a sly grin.

"What is it?" Tiki asked.

Ronde rolled his eyes. "If she told you, what kind of surprise would it be?"

"Hmmph," said Tiki, who loved surprises but couldn't stand the suspense.

"Hey," Ronde said, changing the subject, "can you believe we really made the play-offs, after all we've been through?"

"No doubt," said Tiki. "I thought the season was over when Coach Spangler left."

"Yeah, and I thought we were done after we lost those first two games."

"Me too," Tiki admitted. "We all did. Cody was such a mess, and Coach Wheeler looked so lost . . ."

Ronde laughed and shook his head. "Amazing," he said. "And that was just the first two weeks!"

"I'll tell you," said Tiki, "when they made me the kicker in place of Adam, that was the worst. I knew it was all over!"

"You got that right," Ronde agreed, laughing. "Man, you are a *terrible* kicker!"

"Hey!" Tiki said, suddenly insulted. "I wasn't *that* stinky."

Ronde gave him a look, and they both cracked up.

"Okay. I was that stinky," Tiki said.

"Nah, I'm just playin' with you, man," said Ronde.

They got home, and their mom made them wait in the living room while she went into the kitchen to get their surprise.

Then she came walking out with it—a cake in the shape of a football, with the head of turkey! It had chocolate icing, the twins' favorite, and on it was written, *Play Proud, Eagles!*

"WOW!" the boys said together.

"Mom, that is awesome!" Ronde said.

"Mmm, let's eat!" Tiki said, rubbing his hands together. "I'm hungry for chocolate!"

As they ate together, feeling warm and dry and happy and excited, Ronde said, "Isn't it amazing we made the play-offs, after all those things went wrong?"

"It *is* amazing," Tiki said. "It's totally unreal!"

"And I want you boys to remember every minute of it," said Mrs. Barber. "Every last moment. Because life is going to throw you lots of unexpected challenges and obstacles. Just remember, Tiki and Ronde, you can get through anything, and survive to fight another day, if you believe in yourselves—and if you always, always *play proud.*"

FOOTBALL SIGNALS

1 Ball ready for play
*Untimed down

2 Start clock

3 Time-out
Discretionary or injury
time-out (follow by
tapping hands on
chest)

4 TV/Radio time-out

5 Touchdown
Field goal
Point(s) after touchdown

6 Safety

7 Dead ball foul
Touchback (move side to side)

8 First down

9 Loss of down

10 Incomplete forward pass
Penalty declined
No play, no score
Toss option deferred

11 Legal touching of forward pass or scrimmage kick

12 Inadvertent whistle (Face Press Box)

13 Disregard flag

14 End of period

15 Sideline warning

16 First touching (NFHS) Illegal touching

17 Uncatchable forward pass (NCAA)

18

Encroachment (NFHS)
Offside defense or free-kick defense (NCAA)

19

False start
Illegal formation
Encroachment offense
(NCAA)

20

Illegal shift—2 hands
Illegal motion—1 hand

21

Delay of game

22

Substitution infraction

23

Failure to wear
required equipment

24 Illegal helmet contact

27 Unsportsmanlike conduct
Noncontact foul

28 Illegal participation

29 Sideline interference
(Face Press Box)

30 Running into or
Roughing kicker or
holder

31 Illegal batting/kicking
(Followed by pointing
toward toe for kicking)

*Numbers 25 and 26 are for future signals.

32   Invalid fair catch signal (NFHS) Illegal fair catch signal

33   Forward pass interference Kick catching interference

34   Roughing passer

35   Illegal pass/forward handing (Face Press Box)

36   Intentional grounding

37   Ineligible downfield on pass

38   Personal foul

39   Clipping

40   Blocking below waist
Illegal block

41   Chop block

42   Holding/obstructing
Illegal use of hands/
arms

43   Illegal block in the back

44 Helping runner
Interlocked blocking

45 Grasping face mask
or helmet opening

46 Tripping

47 Disqualification